v

:

ACEPHALIC
IMPERIAL

Damian Murphy is the author of *The Academy Outside of Ingolstadt*, *Seduction of the Golden Pheasant*, *The Exaltation of the Minotaur*, *Daughters of Apostasy* and *The Star of Gnosia*, among other collections and novellas. His work has been published on the Mount Abraxas, Les Éditions de L'Oubli, and L'Homme Récent imprints of Ex Occidente Press, in Bucharest, and by Zagava Books, in Dusseldorf. He was born and lives in Seattle, Washington.

SNUGGLY BOOKS

damian murphy

THE
ACEPHALIC
IMPERIAL

THIS IS A SNUGGLY BOOK

ISBN: 978-1-64525-045-6

THE
ACEPHALIC
IMPERIAL

Séverine shifted her gaze down to the cup she cradled in her hands. Arabesques of red and gold adorned the surface of the fine bone china, the lower flourishes culminating in a ring of double-headed eagles near the rim. The surface of her coffee reflected the radiant glow of the lamp above. She could discern, as well, a fragment of the wallpaper. Its pattern looked different when it was mirrored in the dark black liquid. She felt as if she were peering into another part of the house.

"Did you know," asked the man that sat across from her, "that this was once my father's private office?"

She raised her eyes again to her potential employer. He imparted the impression that he was the last noble scion of a line of trustworthy and honorable men. His clothing was impeccable, his manner was distinguished, yet he was animated by a nervous fire that defiled its containing vessel. He seemed completely cut off from the rest of the world. His isolation clung to him like a shadow.

"I used to creep into the space in the middle of the night while the rest of the household was sleeping," he confessed. "My father was an overly fastidious man, yet he never locked his office door. I'd sit in his chair, savor the scent of his tobacco, and carefully examine the papers on his desk. I sometimes pretended I was an intruder in the house that had found his way into its secret heart."

Séverine slowly rotated her coffee cup between her fingers. Her gaze shifted back and forth between the splendors of the china and the man that sat across from her. She wasn't especially anxious before him. Her desire for the job was only marginal at best. She had no idea how she was expected to respond to his divulgence. It suddenly occurred to her that she couldn't recall his name.

"I did this not so much to undermine my father's authority," he continued, his eyes bathed in shadow. "But rather for the simple reason that I was not supposed to be here. I was compelled by the fact that my act of trespass had never been explicitly forbidden. Of all the pleasures in this world, few are more exquisite than the breaking of a tacit rule."

The man offered his confession as if it were a sacrament which Séverine accepted in kind. When she'd first laid eyes on him, she'd thought him untoward, though she quickly came to understand that this was not the case at all. He was simply given to obsessions that threatened to consume him and it was all he could do to maintain his composure beneath their implacable demands. Séverine was not put off by this. If anything, it roused her curiosity. In truth, she was far more interested in her interviewer than in her prospects for employment.

The man had turned his attention back to one of the papers on the desk before him. For a moment, he seemed impossibly lost in the neatly-lined fields of her official application. "My ad would have you believe that you're applying for a position as a live-in maid," he said. "The wording, I'm afraid, was intentionally ambiguous. For that, I apologize. It simply couldn't be helped." He lifted his gaze again to meet Séverine's. "The truth is that we already have a full-time house cleaner. The role I'm hoping you'll fulfill is of an altogether different nature."

She took another sip of coffee and patiently waited for him to explain his statement. It was abundantly clear that he had not the slightest bit of interest in her previous experience. When she'd agreed to the interview, she'd hardly expected to be chosen for the job. She was hardly suited for this type of position, having only ever worked as a hotel maid. Her employment was spotty. She worked as little as possible. Honest labor interfered with her true vocation, which was to live the life of a dilettante.

"The particularities of the position might be difficult to explain," the man continued, his fingertips lightly touching the document as if to fine-tune the consistency of the ink. "I think my requirements can best be demonstrated by way of a simple exercise. Assuming, of course, this is agreeable?"

"It's agreeable," said Séverine, without a second thought. "I can't think of any reason to object."

Her host regarded her with fastidious eyes, his anticipation gleaming like a precious stone beneath the light. "I'm going to leave the office," he said. "I'll be gone for no more than ten minutes at most. Perhaps a little less. While I'm out, I want you to take something that doesn't belong to you—it can be anything at all. You can put it in your handbag if you'd like, or you can hide it someplace in the office. When I return, I want to see you sitting in your chair exactly as you are now."

An almost sensual excitation arose in the core of Séverine's heart. She found the notion so appealing that she feared her expression would betray her enthusiasm. It was the kind of contrivance only children indulged in and seemed strangely unsuited to the man that conveyed it. It was clear that he sensed her amusement and was pleased with her response.

"I might mention that there are items of considerable worth in this office," he said before rising from his chair. "While they won't by any means be easy to find, I can hardly discourage you from trying. You should know that the value of what you choose is irrelevant to the nature of the task. You're free to do whatever you please while I'm gone. My workplace is in your hands."

A moment's eye-contact was made as if to confirm the terms of their simple agreement before the man proceeded into the corridor and softly closed the door behind him. Séverine remained in her chair for a moment as his footsteps receded. The modest office felt very different without the indwelling presence of its inhabitant. She allowed herself to take in its character as if she were sampling the fragrance of an exotic per-fume. The thought of searching for something of obvi-ous value seemed a futile endeavor. She preferred the prospect of taking something small, something whose absence was trivial and unlikely to be noticed. Her gaze passed over a row of card cabinets and a map chest with brass handles, alighting at last upon the contents of a bookcase that was partially concealed in shadow. The notion that occurred to her was at once perfectly ap-propriate and undeniably perverse.

Rising from her seat, she took herself around the desk and stepped over to the shelf. Forgoing the temp-tation to rifle through the desk drawers, she began a hasty study of the nature and variety of the volumes arrayed before her. Wedged between a humidor and a white marble bust was found a series of thick books bound in pale vellum. An ornamental flourish was stamped in gilt upon each of their spines. No trace of a title or even a volume number could be seen on any one of them. She was certain that she'd found what she was looking for. Within seconds, she'd chosen one from early in the series and laid it flat upon the surface of the desk.

The front and back covers revealed little more than a pair of marbled boards beyond the vellum. No author, title, or table of contents were found on the inside. The body of the text began abruptly on the first page and was divided into several sections, each with its own heading in capital letters. The initial paragraph began mid-sentence, appearing to continue directly from the volume before it. The font was inflexible and fairly austere. The pages weren't numbered and the margins were wide. She scarcely had time to scan a single passage before her interviewer's impending return. THE ASSASSINATION OF THE PORTER read a heading on the left-side page, followed by THE NIGHT OF THE PEACOCK and FROM THE IVORY TO THE ABSOLUTE. While she desperately wanted to sit at the desk and explore the pages to follow, this would accomplish little more than her being apprehended in the act.

She hesitated for a moment as her fingers rested on the page, not entirely certain whether she wanted to commit to an act that couldn't be undone. In her mind, the possibility comprised a sort of test—not for her, but for her potential employer. She briefly contemplated the notion of worth and the value of the irreplaceable. At last, fearing that her time was running out, she flipped to a page a little later in the book and ripped it clean from its bindings.

The ease with which the sheet came free surprised her. The thought of creasing the paper caused her definite anxiety, yet in the name of expedience she folded it in half and slipped it into her handbag. She replaced the book and returned to the safety of her chair on the other side of the desk, her face flush with the thrill of having committed a minor act of vandalism. A further sip of her now-tepid coffee seemed officially to seal the act.

Now that the deed had been accomplished, she was able to relax and explore the office a little for its own sake. Her attention was attracted to a small framed photograph that hung on the far side of the entrance. She hadn't noticed it before, as the door had been open and had concealed it from view. A man was shown in full military dress beneath the four flaming bulbs of a hanging lamp. A modest assemblage of stars and medals shone like emblems of the prophet on the breast of his uniform. An arch of finely-crafted stonework was visible behind him. She could just make out the bottom of an ornamental rail. His mathematical gaze and pedantic bearing left no question as to his identity. As she looked upon his younger self, Séverine was suddenly able to remember his name. She said it once beneath her breath so that she wouldn't forget it again: *Vital*.

Like the undying spirit of a fallen king, the pronouncement of his name appeared to summon the man himself. The sound of his approaching footsteps on the stairs below gave rise to a trace of apprehension. Séverine fretted that he'd express displeasure at her choice. She'd intentionally gone too far, crossing right over the line that he'd unofficially drawn for her. At the same time, her transgression felt perfectly justified. It was intended not as an affront, but as a reasonable tactic. He had, after all, instantiated this game. He'd even encouraged her to try to break the rules. Her concerns were dispersed as the man returned to his seat. They regarded one another like confidants beneath the golden effusion of the lamps. Séverine's handbag lay on the edge of the desk, having been carefully positioned precisely as it was before. Vital didn't so much as spare it a momentary glance.

"There's little else that I'm inclined to tell you," he said, as if, by merely remaining in the office, she'd passed his little test. "The job is not a laborious one, yet you'll be given enough to keep you occupied. There will be no explanations as to the reasoning behind your tasks. You are to report directly to me and to no one else. I can assure you that nothing salacious or improper will ever be expected of you." The fact that he would mention this at all was suspect, yet somehow Séverine felt him incapable of lechery. He seemed wholly deficient in that particular regard, as if his appetites had long since withered beneath the weight of his indifference. "Do you suppose you could work under such conditions?" he asked after a momentary pause.

Séverine had to force herself to wait before assenting. She couldn't think of a single proposition that would appeal to her more. No salary had been mentioned, but she hardly cared about that. A pittance in addition to room and board would suffice, just enough to make the occasional purchase and save up for the eventuality of moving on. "I think so," she said at last. "I think it will prove satisfactory."

"It pleases me to hear this," said Vital, moving the paper before him to one side. "Your room will be ready in one week's time. I'll have you notified when everything's arranged and you can start immediately after."

Séverine's eyes were drawn once again to the cup that rested in the shadow of her handbag. The two-headed birds appeared like fiery wardens around the upper section just below the rim. The tips of their wings, which crossed over one another, resembled writhing flames with fine-tipped points. Had Vital expected her to be so unimaginative as to put the cup into her handbag? The thought of making so obvious a choice had never even occurred to her.

Here begins my descent into something for which I have no words. Not as yet, anyway. I have scarcely the slightest clue what lies ahead of me. It may be nothing of particular interest, but at least I'll have someplace compelling to sleep. While this house is not tremendously large, it's a fortress compared to what I'm used to.

My own room is located off of a rarely-used dining hall in the upper story of the house. Not a single window relieves its overwhelming intimacy. The decorations are more than adequate. The dimensions suit my temperament. Already, I feel as if the room belongs to me. It serves its purpose as an autonomous enclave within the larger territory of the manor.

A few items of furniture warrant mention. My narrow bed, which is wholly unremarkable, lies in the center of the room against the back wall. Directly opposite, a few paces from the foot, hangs a convex oval mirror. The bulbous glass is framed in intricate black lacquer topped with a finely-sculpted eagle. Two heads extend to the right and to the left above its outstretched wings. The term is 'bicephalic' if I'm not mistaken. I noticed a similar motif during my interview. The mirror is flanked by two wall-mounted lamps of common, if elegant design, their upturned bowls of amber glass providing the sole official source of light. They look like miniature suns in reflection on the curved sides of the mirror. The heads of the eagle are trained directly above them.

Nightstands stand to either side of the headboard, one bearing a statuette and the other a mantle clock. I've since appropriated both of them for use elsewhere. My hopes were dashed, upon looking in their drawers, to find them perfectly empty. I'd hoped to discover a loaded pistol, a phial of poison, or at least a misplaced key. Given the nature of my initial duties, I'll soon have no shortage of items to fill them with.

My official uniforms, along with my tattered Chinese bathrobe, are concealed behind the doors of an antique armoire. Carved panels, tall and slender, allow a limited view of its interior. I've pushed the clothes to either side and set a candle on the bottom. The shadows projected through the elaborations of the screen roll like geometric angels across my ceiling. The inside is so spacious that there's little danger that I'll set my clothes on fire.

The candle was taken from the top of the armoire. I've replaced it with the handful of volumes that comprise my personal library. They're currently wedged between the bust and the clock that I've taken from the nightstands. Never once have I bothered to catalog my collection. I keep it pitiably modest. For the sake of completeness, I'll do so here:

> A book of poems by Robert Desnos and another by St. John of the Cross
> *The Most Holy Trinosophia* of the Comte de St. Germain
> John Ruskin's *Seven Lamps of Architecture*
> The Wilhelm/Baynes *I-Ching*
> Three volumes, not consecutive, of the *Cantos* of Ezra Pound
> *The Secret Order of Assassins*, on the hashish-eating murderers of Persia and Syria
> *Buch Abramelin*—alas, in German—I cannot read a word of it
> *On Isis and Osiris* from Plutarch's *Moralia*
> A book on Assyrian priest-kings
> A series of mystical visions transcribed by the self-styled 'Great Beast' himself

With literature, as with every facet of my life, I tend to proceed with reckless abandon. I hold to no fixed plan or organization. My choice of reading material is as arbitrary as the wind. My only rule is that for each book acquired, another must be disposed of. In an ideal world, I would own no more than a single, slender volume. I would commit the whole of its contents to memory and keep it purely as a talisman.

Onward now to more essential things. I've already been given my first few directives, as Vital prefers to call them. We've had exactly one official meeting after he showed me to my lodgings. I couldn't help but notice that there's still no lock upon his office door. No tour of the house was given nor do I think one will be forthcoming. I suspect he prefers that I explore the place on my own. He's given me only the essential instructions I'll need to carry out my tasks. The rest, I suppose, is up to my ingenium.

The first thing I was shown was a circle of dark glass in a little-used closet just down the hall from my bedroom. When I put my face up to its surface, I could see directly into Vital's office. The other side is a mirror set into a shallow niche in the wall. The view afforded is fairly comprehensive—the desk, the cabinets, the map chest, and the bookshelf all lie fully exposed to the hidden observer. All of this is tainted with a deep shade of crimson that obscures the fine details. Had I been watched during my interview as I ripped the page from Vital's book? I'm certain I heard him depart down the stairway after passing through the door. There may be another means of reaching the closet, or perhaps his wife, Agata, observed me through the glass. For all I know, I may have been watched by the maid.

My principal task, as irrational as it seems, is to spy on Vital through the mirror while he's working in the office. I'm to do this for no less than an hour a day, taking care to vary my schedule so as to keep it as unpredictable as possible. I'm to take notes on anything I deem appropriate—anything at all. Most importantly, I'm not to allow myself to be apprehended as I do this, either by Vital or by anybody else. I'm told this will be fairly easy, as the surrounding rooms and corridors are rarely used by anyone but he.

In addition, I'm to keep an occasional eye on Isabel, the maid, and to keep regular notes on her activities and habits. It's been stressed that I must be as furtive as I can, that it's best if she doesn't suspect my activities. Vital doesn't seem to think that this will pose me any challenge. My reports need not be detailed. I can watch her from a distance.

"It's not that I suspect she's stepping out of line or that she's failing in her duties," he assured me. "Your goal is not to catch her in an act of indolence or disobedience. Merely make yourself familiar with her mannerisms and routines. You might make a special study of the routes she follows through the house, for example. Any additional details are entirely up to you."

Further, I've been encouraged to pilfer the occasional trivial object—doorstops, serving spoons, eyeglass cases and other such minor things.

At all hours of the day and night, unless I've been specifically instructed not to, I'm to wear the same style of uniform required of Isabel—a cross between a maid's outfit and a church-woman's dress. Meals are taken three times a day. I'll find them waiting for me in the kitchen. I'm permitted to take my provisions to my room, but either way I'm to eat alone. We're to meet once a week, my employer and I, at which time I'm to relate to him anything I deem worth telling. It's been made clear that I'll be given further directives based on my performance of the ones I've completed.

Vital remains impeccably congenial in every aspect of his role. I suspect that the terms of my employment are known only between the two of us. I can't help but regard him as a fetishist—his obsessions, while harmless, are anything but hidden. The indiscretions he's assigned me are so minor that I almost wonder if he's joking. As negligible as they are, they have an urgency about them, an unmistakable momentousness that I can't quite put my finger on. They're like the cast-off husks of cardinal sins.

The majority of the house is still completely unfamiliar to me. It feels as if I'm living in a foreign country, complete with customs, protocols, and a history of its own. From the moment I set foot here, I've been aware of a particular mystique, a subtle thread of intoxication that courses through the rooms and corridors. It travels with the pulse of an electrical charge, collecting in the door frames and stairways. It seems to emanate from the house itself like a silent, yet sonorous song. I can almost taste its tenuous vibration. It has a distinctly metallic flavor. Its effect is at once narcotic and enlivening.

While this unseen force is notably amplified in the presence of my employer, it rises to a fever pitch whenever Agata comes near. Thus far, I've encountered the latter only briefly and in passing. She regards me as if she hasn't quite decided what to do with me. If Vital comes off as a master locksmith, his wife is more akin to a battering ram. She's like an inferno, that woman. I'm a little bit afraid of her. I'm convinced she could destroy me with a single, well-placed glance.

This entry cannot be considered complete without a transcript of the page I stole from Vital's book. I've held off on reading it for over a week, preferring to wait until I was settled in to examine it in detail. I haven't the slightest inkling what it is—a novel? A confession? A sort of epic, rambling poem? The text has the quality of an incantation or a fragment from a dream. Vital has yet to ask for it back and I don't think that he will, yet I feel I'd better copy down its contents just in case. There are other advantages to doing so. In writing it down, the influence of the passages will be absorbed into my blood. I've been keeping the page beneath the candle in the interior of my armoire. In my mind, the flame draws its essence up into the chamber of the wardrobe before projecting it out onto the ceiling while I sleep.

The style of writing bears witness to certain aspects of Vital's personality. The text is inexplicably tied to him. It seems to reverse his dispositions like a mirror image. I can't help but think of the photograph I'd found in his office during my interview. The references to Verdun and Pozières would seem to date it to the years of the First World War. This accords with Vital's probable age—I'd place him in his late fifties. What follows is an exact transcription of the content of both sides of the page.

as with a desiccated flower. The starlings launch into sudden flight, disappearing down a stairwell. The mathematical sequence is carefully worked out and etched into the mirror. The numbers form a simple cipher based on the alignment of presiding winds. We chant our incantations as we consecrate the iron. The bells are rung with great solemnity. The fumigations are set aflame. After a rigorous evening of ceaseless labor, the working space is prepared.

The Transition to the Heart of Night

We take the graphite in hand and set the torches aflame. The heat is stifling in the watchtower. Receivers are aimed at invisible signals like the mouths of ancient oracles. The atmosphere shifts with a flip in the numeric sequence. We hear an audible hum and feel a palpable magnetic flux. The onset, as always, is a little bit disorienting. There's a numbness of the tongue and flashing lights behind the eyes. Our senses are eclipsed by a succession of images as we lose touch with our surroundings. We collectively dream of an old hotel in the heart of a nameless, Prussian winter.

The Impending Disaster

Visions of silken upholstery and the décolleté of a reclining countess. Debauchery on seats of alabaster as the lamps blaze in the hotel lobby. A tide pool of black ink expands within the heart of the concierge. A provocateur attempts to disrupt a gathering of the elect. Arrangements are made beneath timeless influences at once regal and debased. The concierge conceives a plan of impotent revenge. A concealed message passed by hand beneath the pregnant chandeliers. A sense of the catastrophe to come.

The Scent of Infamy

The visions intensify and the colors grow more vivid. Rivers of narrative flow in reverse. The hotel is tainted with scandal after a case of mistaken identity. A society dinner is brought to ruin as a canary is set loose inside the dining hall. A pamphlet found in a handbag and a note slipped under a hotel room door. Loyalties are shattered and allegiances are interchanged. A saboteur is identified, yet the countess has absconded. The chaplain is found naked in a recess of the pantry, his poisoned prayer-book soaking in a bathtub in the dark. A trail of invisible ink leads to the body of the concierge. A second plan is conceived involving a decoy in the cellar. The hotel registry is daubed with lamp oil and ceremonially set aflame, its entries unraveling like tattered strands of ghostly, crimson thread.

A Message from the Front

Reception breaks up and the narrative fades out again. We return to ourselves before the flicker of torchlight. Interference somewhere in the line between one station and another. The experiment is not entirely a failure—the results are far from insignificant. We'll try again, but first we must wait for more favorable conditions. The watchtower fills with pungent clouds of imported tobacco. We raise our glasses of white Rioja among the never-ending stink of kerosene. The festive atmosphere is brought to a halt by the delivery of a message: a fiasco in Verdun precedes a bombardment at Pozières.

THE RAVISHING OF THE MIRROR
The following morning we begin preparations for yet another undertaking. The series is endless. We embrace the repetition. We begin our recitations as the sun comes up. The results are distributed differently this time. By noon the winds will have diverted in their courses. The starlings have abandoned us and the watchtower is desolate. Hardly have we positioned the device

15 January

In the three days that I've been here, I've been able to determine a single thing of indisputable significance: there's nothing quite so fascinating as watching Vital through the two-way glass. He does little but work, so far as I can tell, though I can't nearly make out what he's working on. I don't think it has anything to do with the series of books lined up on the shelves behind him. I've witnessed neatly-typed documents, hand-written forms, and papers so old that the print has nearly faded. He engages with these things as if immersed in a mesmeric trance.

His fingers scan the rows and columns with the deftness and strategy of a military expedition. He attacks and withdraws, advances and retreats, all with painstaking deliberation and meticulous care. He does these things so slowly that I have to wonder at his efficiency. The attention that he lavishes on the minutest of details rivals that of a master craftsman, combining the veneration of a man of the cloth with the shrewdness of a thief. All the while, I can't help but feel that the whole thing is merely an exercise, as if he's buying time to avoid attending to the real work at hand.

Isabel has proven to be every bit as captivating as her employer. Her eccentricities have all the practiced intricacy of finely-honed routines. The most significant among them is her habit of stealing items of dubious utility: hairbrushes, sequins, and quantities of salt, among other things. Though she takes few steps to avoid detection, I somehow don't imagine this is part of her official job. I suspect she does this purely for her own amusement.

There are a host of other peculiarities as well. I'm given the impression that she regards the house itself as an object of sensual interest. She's incapable of wiping down the banisters, for instance, without running her fingers along the wooden surface afterward. The way she caresses the windowsills suggests an erotic disposition toward the material itself. What she does with the lampshades can hardly be described—while it doesn't quite approach the lurid, it's definitely conspicuous. So far as I can tell, she regards even the carpets as worthy of her adoration. Earlier today, I watched her lightly brush her finger over the surface of a keyhole. Though I was watching from behind, she seemed to treat the copper ridges as if they were the lips of her beloved.

Unlike with Vital's rigorous self-restraint, there's a lightheartedness to her activities. I've wondered more than once whether she knows she's being watched. Whatever the case, I note it down without comment or critique. I've omitted her penchant for theft, on the other hand. Somehow, I feel it would comprise a betrayal to report this particular act.

Despite the diligent performance of my official directives, I still have lengthy spans of time at my disposal. There's something especially gratifying about lingering around the house with so little to do. Vital has encouraged me to make my presence known here, to allow myself to be frequently seen among the ostentatious furnishings. I've considered the possibility that what he really wants is a scandal, that he hopes that word will spread that he's taken a much younger lover and passed her off as a second maid. Perhaps he's using me to compel his wife to ask for a divorce. The two of them have such little contact that they hardly seem married at all.

I spent several hours yesterday afternoon simply sitting in a wicker chair in the downstairs parlor. In time, I'll grow bored with my abundance of idleness, but for now it's a luxury I wouldn't trade for anything. The pleasure of letting time drip away without the slightest concern is like a precious liqueur. I feel as if I'm afforded all the pleasures of laudanum without the attendant depravity.

Behind me, on the mantelpiece, next to a vase overflowing with winter orchids, stood a sizable iron urn engraved with military scenes from a bygone empire. A gilt-framed mirror on the opposing wall allowed me to casually examine it without rising from my seat. The urn is topped with a double-headed eagle—the motif is found with surprising frequency in all quarters of the house. Before I left the room I took a single orchid from the vase, lifted the lid of the ostentatious item, and dropped it into the empty bowl. I couldn't hope for a better place to stash the household objects I've been instructed to pilfer.

I'm increasingly moved to devote considerable effort to a careful study of Agata. She imparts an astringency as venomous as any toxin, a vehemence of temper that both corrupts and resurrects. Her presence can be likened to a rolling wave of static that sweeps through the corridors from one end to the other. A high-pitched wail, just barely discernible, seems to follow in her wake. This is not so much heard as it's felt within the body. I've experienced this just enough to be assured of its consistency.

The woman proceeds from room to room according to a fairly fixed route. It's clear that she's a creature of habit. She comports herself like a queen in chess. The stoutness of her body and the severity of her mien impart the impression of an abbess. Her imposing appearance perfectly complements the outdated luxuriance of the house—the faux-religious imagery, the military pretenses, the overstated nostalgia so typical of her and Vital's generation. I'm supposed to be trailing Isabel, yet the matron of the house is far more interesting. I feel that I'd best step lightly lest I incur the weight of her contempt.

I spend my evenings safely locked up in the confines of my secluded little chamber. Here, the house's innate essence takes on ambiguous and unfamiliar properties. As the hour grows late, I'm given to a feeling that could almost be described as a low fever. At first I thought I'd caught some minor illness, but the symptoms, when examined, are anything but disagreeable. Rather than the depression of energy that accompanies sickness, this flush gives rise to a subtle flame that courses all throughout my body. Pale arabesques take form in the back of my mind, their traceries illuminated by a persistent inner glow. The phenomenon is so elusive that it quickly fades to nothing beneath even the slightest degree of scrutiny.

Already, my private quarters have become my refuge and my home. The candle in my armoire has burned nearly two-thirds of the way down. I'll see if I can find another one to replace it with tomorrow. As the height of the flame descends by imperceptible degrees, the surging play of light and shadow slowly drifts across my ceiling. The flickering lattices create a hallucinatory theater that threatens to infiltrate the walls of sleep.

19 January

I've been intending to write another entry for at least a couple of days. I'm insufferably lazy and my role in the house has done little to discourage my lamentable habits. I've just had my first official meeting with Vital. He seemed inordinately pleased as he read over my hastily scribbled notes. Though he didn't say a word about them one way or another, I was left with the impression that my performance has been more than adequate.

When asked how I'd been taking to the job, I kept my answer brief, knowing that my natural reticence is invaluable to my place here. I don't think Vital has any desire to know what's on my mind, nor does he wish to pierce the veil in which I keep myself enshrouded. The less he knows about my feelings, the more I can be of service. Likewise, the uncertainties regarding my position allow me to work with an impartiality that would be otherwise impossible.

A couple of new directives were given me and several suggestions ambiguously dropped. Most significantly, I'm to shift my sleeping schedule, rising much later in the day and remaining awake into the night. The house is to become entirely my own while its inhabitants are sleeping. I can go where I please, do what I want, and generally have the run of the place so long as I don't wake anyone. In addition, I've been instructed to alter the hours I spend inside the closet. I'm no longer to look through the glass in the evening while Vital's working in his office, but rather late at night when he's asleep.

The prospect of observing an uninhabited room seems to border on the absurd. This is the first task I've been given that has no plausible explanation. The tacit assumption I've held up to this point was that my work was meant to gratify the fetishes of an unimportant man. Though I knew this not to be strictly true, it's allowed me to maintain the illusion of coherence. While it's possible that Vital derives some kind of pleasure from doling out irrational tasks, I suspect his motives are far more obscure than this. The more I try to understand his agenda, the more baffled I become.

As I leaned back in my chair with my teacup in my hands, I found my gaze continually drifting to the unlabeled books lined up behind my employer. While these are technically visible through the two-way glass, the darkness of the lens renders them impossibly obscure. I made the decision, as I examined them from afar, to creep into the office and rip out a second page. I don't know why I hadn't thought of this before. I've gone over the first page again and again while in the sanctuary of my room. The pilfered item itself still resides beneath the candlestick in my armoire. Before the sun rises tomorrow, it will have a companion.

My perception of Vital has notably changed since I've taken on the role of voyeur. I suspect I'll truly miss this part of my position. One feels a certain intimacy with a person after watching them do nothing for several hours. I feel that a bond has formed between us, though it's perfectly stoic and devoid of affection. This is probably as close as I'll ever come to truly knowing my employer. The gulf he imposes between himself and the world is simply too wide to traverse. He's like a man that lives in exile from the empire of his senses.

In that regard, I often wonder about Vital's relationship with Agata. I rarely see them in each other's company, nor do I detect the slightest trace of warmth between them. They sleep in separate bedrooms and they never take their meals together—Vital eats in his office while Agata sits alone at the dining room table. I get the impression that years of familiarity have yielded little but contempt. I suppose these are the common signs of the ravages of marriage.

Already my days seem to blur together like a syphilitic's languorous dream. Such is the euphoria attendant to my service that I pass from room to room as if in an opiated trance. I haven't set foot outside of doors from the day that I moved in. Come to think of it, so far as I can tell neither has Isabel or Agata. The cook sees to the shopping (I still don't know his name). He's scarcely here more than a few hours a day. Vital makes occasional excursions to God knows where. For all I know, the world outside has been reduced to a smoldering ruin.

I can say without the slightest doubt that Isabel is well-aware she's being watched. Her antics have grown progressively erratic with each passing day. She's taken to speaking in furtive whispers to the hanging chandeliers, tracing hidden patterns along the wallpaper with the tips of her middle and ring-fingers, and kneeling before the heating vents with her head bowed down as if in fervent prayer. Her mannerisms lack the manic obsession of the truly neurotic. She contorts her body in a mockery of eroticism that speaks to the fact that she's putting on a show. I feel obliged to play back, to turn her games around upon her in a particularly baffling manner. A plan is beginning to take form in my mind. I'll make my move either tomorrow or the next day.

There is little else of note to report. The iron urn in the parlor is nearly a third of the way filled. Thus far, aside from the initial orchid, I've dropped a variety of items into its interior. Among them are six hand-rolled cigarettes found in the top shelf of an unused cupboard in the pantry. These I boldly stole before the eyes of the cook as he prepared the evening meal. Other items of note include a silver napkin ring, a box of matches to accompany the cigarettes, and a stopper deftly removed from a bottle of aged Burgundy. I've also thrown in some playing cards removed from a small cache of decks found in a dresser drawer. I don't know how often people play cards in this place. Perhaps nobody will notice.

At present, I recline against the foot of my bed awaiting the hour when the household goes to sleep.

My plan is to remain awake until I can stand it no longer. I've spent an hour perusing the platitudes of Ruskin and thrown a perfectly ambiguous I-Ching. Perhaps I'll take a book beneath the lamps of the dining hall or maybe rifle through some drawers before heading to the closet. There's not a scrap of work for me to attend to, nothing overly pressing that lies before me. I'm perfectly content in my insouciance. Even the experience of boredom is exquisite in this place.

An offhand comment dropped by Vital still reverberates in the back of my mind. "You're afforded freedoms in this house that lie entirely beyond my grasp," he stated. "Can you imagine how foolish I'd appear were I to spy on my own housecleaner, engage in acts of petty theft, or lounge about for hours on end for no other reason than the pleasure of doing so? At this point in my life, I can scarcely spend an idle minute without the nagging feeling that I should be attending to some needful task. People of my stature need to live vicariously. We should all be so lucky to have employed somebody as versatile as yourself."

Vital has a tendency to speak like an oracle. His most trivial remarks are imbued with subtle meanings and perplexing insinuations. Taken at face value, what he said sounds very pretty, but I'm certain that there's more to our arrangement than that. The trace of humor in his statement makes it perfectly clear that there's something he's not letting on. What's more, I have a feeling that I may never find out what it is.

My minor mission was accomplished without the slightest bit of difficulty. Rather than linger in the office, I got what I was looking for and immediately escaped. I'd just spent a perfectly listless hour gazing aimlessly through the back of the mirror. By the time I breached the unlocked door, the contours of the space had nearly burned themselves into my mind. Still they reside as a backdrop to my thoughts, the highlights and shadows persisting in a deep red haze. It feels as if the place is inside of me now, as if I could somehow turn inward and inhabit it.

The following is transcribed from a single page torn from a volume a little later in the series than the last one.

appropriated from a doctrine of insur-rection. An imminent revolt among the registrars' wives beneath the banners of the Emperor. Scandalous rites among the daughters of nobility in a chamber under-ground. The impending resurrection of the concierge and all that it portends.

THE ERUPTION OF NIGHT
A fire in the embassy. The flow of pitch along the palace stairs. The seduction of the monarchy and a courthouse in ruins. The rites of violation and the perfume of imperium. An explosion in the citadel

and the immersion of the scepter. The torches blush like concubines amidst the desecrated city. The countess unveiled in the embrace of the night. Her adversary barricaded in the basement of a church. The geometry of mirrors and the doubling of sin. The sovereign seal across the heart of the porter as he's pushed over the precipice. A glimpse of the names in the hotel registry before it was destroyed. A forgotten dispatch of mutinous angels in the symmetries of the wallpaper. A flaming candle set before a mirror in the dark. The overwhelming scent of royalty and the inversion of the crown. A throne in the invisible and the reflection of the star. A double-headed eagle in a closet in the garret. A banner with the emblems of the Acephalic Imperial.

A LITANY OF DISCONTENT

A hint of a pattern begins to emerge in the sequence of heraldic arms. An emissary sets out upon a perilous excursion into the heart of the machine. A progressive descent through a radiant earth steeped in spectral emanations. A meeting among legates in a secret court and the expulsion of the peacock. The strangling of the sentinels in an antechamber filled with owls. A divulgence of iniquity in scathing, scarlet ink. The drawing of lots. The implosion of the signal. A lapse in the connection. The end of the transmission.

The Veil of Oblivion

The Return to the Front
We wake to timeless monotony and inexplicable shame like sailors debauched by the vastness of the sea. With sufficient exposure comes a type of immodesty more languorous than any opiate, its inexcusable fires consuming all ambition and

redeeming every trace of pain. Our senses have been ravished by insatiable desires, our uniforms soaked through with sweat. Copper wire consolidates the imprint in the aether. We're left with tantalizing fragments of a message from the source. Our position is precarious; the front lines have advanced. Pending further orders

My dreams last night were visited by an eagle with no head—a herald, perhaps, of the Acephalic Imperial. If the two-headed eagle looks out upon a double world, one of them visible and the other one concealed, the acephalic eagle fixes its gaze upon a place that can't be reached by either of them. There's something to this notion that I feel in my body but which I can't quite grasp with my mind. Only the sovereign without a head is truly fit to wear the crown.

I'm reminded of a fragment of Greek ritual I'd once perused in which a series of poetic incantations are delivered to "The Headless One", an omnipotent god whose virtues are extolled by barbarous names and majestic attributions. The *Acéphale review* of Georges Bataille & co. also comes to mind. The motif has always intrigued me, though I've scarcely given it nearly the consideration that it's due.

A far more pressing matter is at hand: I've instantiated contact with the maid. We spent an evening sipping Vital's brandy over several hands of Écarté and conversing in my private room. I've been informed that

I'm a miserable spy. In the brusque words of my new confidant, I 'step as lightly as a horse'. Isabel, as I'd suspected, has been putting on a show for me. I managed to amuse her with a counter-performance involving a pair of peacock feathers and a silver serving dish.

Upon stepping through the door, she headed straight for the books lined up on top of my armoire. She didn't even seem to notice the light of the candle that flames inside the cabinet. She professed her love of Ezra Pound and gave a passing nod to Crowley, though the true gems of my collection were entirely ignored. I suppose it's encouraging that she was able to identify so much as a single volume. I, for my part, have managed to discern the seed and root of her every desire. She wants to slip beneath the surface of the visible world and stake her claim on its foundation. While her motives are admirable, her reach is relatively shallow.

Several items of definite interest were conveyed to me over the tops of the cards. I suspect that she was testing me, attempting to deduce something of my character through a careful observation of my method of play. "You're not the first person Vital's hired for this particular position," she said as she removed a number of cards from the deck that were irrelevant to the game. "So far, nobody's lasted for much longer than a week." I found myself wondering if she'd had this exact same conversation with several of my predecessors. "I'd tell you what's expected of you, but the fact is I don't have a clue myself," she continued. "Vital will never breathe a word about it, though of course I haven't asked him."

I was given the impression that I've taken to the job with far more enthusiasm than the others. "They were so put off by the nature of their duties that they were afraid to make the slightest move," said Isabel. "Given their past experience, they were probably well-versed in the arts of stealing and spying. The prospect of doing so with full permission must have terrified them. Their intimidation made them overly talkative. They told me everything that Vital had given them to do. His instructions differ slightly from person to person, though the basics are more or less the same." I wondered aloud how many women were interviewed that didn't make the cut. She guessed at least a dozen in the time that she'd been there, if not significantly more.

Isabel's theory, which is the soul of simplicity, is that Vital is merely tremendously bored. He can think of no better way to amuse himself than to hire a succession of inexperienced young women and submit them to a process that has no rational explanation. "He aims for nothing more than the systematic derangement of your senses," she maintained. I'm sure she knew damn well that she was quoting Rimbaud. She obviously thinks herself an intellectual. The depth and complexity of my position escapes her. Of course, she doesn't know about the series of books I'd found in Vital's office, though I suspect if she did she'd find a way to account for them as well.

The most significant revelation she bestowed upon me involves Agata. I can't quite remember if Vital had specifically referred to her as his wife at some point or if I'd merely inferred as much. As it turns out, they're not husband and wife at all, but siblings. I must admit, this came as somewhat of a shock to me. While the resemblance is slight, it is nonetheless discernible. Neither of them ever married so far as Isabel is aware. As for the house, it's been passed down from father to son for several generations. "There are obvious tensions between the two of them, though it's clear that he defers to her in matters of importance," Isabel pointed out. "Whether she warrants it or not, she always has the upper hand. She absolutely terrified your predecessors."

Not a single guest has set foot in the premises for well over a year, so I'm informed. "From what I've gathered, Agata used to be the queen of the salon. She hosted well-attended séances or spiritist meetings or some such nonsense. These days, she never entertains. She hardly ever even leaves the house. I sometimes wonder if something's happened to her, if she's suffered some trauma that's made her mentally deficient."

I couldn't help but notice that Isabel's company seemed to cut right through the subtle force that interpenetrates the house. She slips through its grasp like a thief in broad daylight, her natural incognizance making her immune to its allures. The effect appears to be passed on to me so long as I remain in her presence, though the familiar symptoms return once I'm alone again. She seems to function like a psychic drain, depleting the attraction of the house's secret fire without suspecting its existence.

Toward the end of our encounter, our conversation turned to the relative merits of our respective positions. "My work is entirely unsupervised," she said, as if I hadn't noticed. "Neither Agatha nor Vital interferes with me and I certainly don't bother them. I'm sure you're aware that I hardly dust. I keep the house just barely presentable. I work whatever hours that I damn well please and I've yet to receive a single complaint. It's a tremendous relief to live under such tolerant conditions. This is by far the easiest job I've ever had."

Within a couple of hours after Isabel had left, I stepped out to fulfill my nightly shift behind the mirror. Vital had long since gone to bed. The office was as empty as the nave of an abandoned church. The monotony of peering at the crimson-drenched enclosure has a tendency to produce a type of physical dissociation. By the time an hour has passed I feel a thousand miles from my body—an effect which gradually diminishes as the night wears on. Tonight, as I stood in the closet with my face before the glass, I was given to a certainty that the room I was observing couldn't possibly coincide with the interior of Vital's office. The sensation became so acute that I was compelled to step out and investigate.

It's possible that my conviction arose from the sheer tedium of my task. In any case, it's not as if my view was any different than it had been before. A trip down the hall and around the corner took me into the office itself. The space looked identical to the one I'd been gazing at, save for the absence of the crimson tint. I even went so far as to step back into the hall to assure myself of the relative position of the two locations. Everything was as it should be, and yet, when I returned to my station, I was again convinced that something was amiss.

Out of persistence, boredom, or an innate streak of insubordination, I returned to the office once more.

Two things competed with equal weight for my attention upon stepping through the door. The first was the temptation to spend the remainder of the night perusing the unmarked series of books. I wanted nothing less than to drown within them, to let their mysteries consume me. The urge was so overwhelming that I could barely restrain myself. Prudence compelled me to stay my hand. I decided it best to leave them alone for the time being. Nevertheless, they continued to tempt me like a cache of precious jewels.

In addition, I was troubled by the feeling that I was being watched. I was given to the unshakable notion that someone else had taken my place behind the mirror. What's more, I imagined that the person in the closet was none other than myself. The familiar affinity I felt with my observer was unmistakable. I had to physically force myself to step over to the mirror and press my face against the wrong side of the lens. Unlike with other two-way mirrors, I could see nothing of the space concealed beyond. This did little to allay my conviction, nor did it relieve me of my feeling of exposure. It's a peculiar sensation to be rendered defenseless by the inquisitive eye of one's self. No other glance could ever be so pitiless, nor so intolerably intimate. This must be akin to the humility felt by the pious before the scrutiny of their god.

Whatever may or may not have been taking place, I decided that I'd worked enough for the night. Ignoring the impulse to pilfer yet another page, feeling not quite finished with the last one, I switched out the office light and returned to the safety and privacy of my room. There, my apprehensions vanished without a trace.

Again I reside at the foot of my bed, the two pages that I've pilfered still concealed in my armoire. In bringing them together, I combine their effect, intermingling their respective characters. Their conjoined souls are forced into this world by the irresistible draw of the flame. The phrases that march like mesmerized savants across the surface of the pages taint the air in my bedroom like a voluptuous perfume. I can scarcely think of a more desirable soporific.

24 January

I'm writing this entry from a forbidden place in which
I've been specifically instructed to reside. Earlier this
evening, Vital called an impromptu meeting in his
office. He casually ignored me for the better part of
twenty minutes as he inspected the details of what appeared to be an expense report. What at last he gave
me the benefit of his attention, he seemed almost surprised that I was there. He proceeded to apprise me
of an unexpected development. "Agata, as it happens,
will be spending the night away from her bedroom,"
he informed me as if the importance of the matter was
self-evident. "She won't return at any point during the
course of the night," he continued. "She'll be holding
vigil in the lower observatory until sunrise at the very
least."

I haven't the slightest clue where the lower observatory might be located, though my suspicion is that
Vital simply made it up. His subtle sense of humor is as
elusive as the moon. He went on to instruct me to hold
a vigil of my own in Agata's private room. As usual, I
was given no indication as to what I was supposed to do

there. I feel certain that my actions, to the degree they can be known, will be monitored, considered, weighed, and duly judged. So far, my tenure in this place has had the flavor of a trial, save for the fact that the outcome seems to carry no consequences whatsoever.

Vital assured me that I need not worry about the prospect of being caught. "If, against all odds, she apprehends you in her bedroom, you won't be held accountable," he said. "Agata is well aware of our arrangement. Any grievances she has will be addressed to me alone. On the other hand, I would greatly prefer that she doesn't know you've been there. You must take care to keep all evidence of your presence to a minimum."

I was given the specific order to remain awake above all else. Anything I lay my hands on must be put back exactly as it was before. I'm to be out of the room by sunrise, though the longer I stay the better. My occupation began at midnight. Vital himself made sure the door was unlocked well before my arrival.

Just to make things interesting, I tore another page from one of Vital's books on my way down here. I've read through the text two times already, though I hesitate to transcribe it just yet. Something tells me it's important that I do so only in the privacy of my own room. While the content is similar in style and character to the others in my possession, there's a trace of something else as well, a foreign element that makes me wonder if it wasn't written by a different hand. It was taken from a place a little later in the series than the other two. The prose has been elevated, the structure made more subtle, the narrative given to open contradictions at once baffling and perfectly appropriate. To judge from these excerpts, the entire text proceeds like a steadily building symphony, complete with developing motifs, recurrent themes, and melodic variations.

A few words must be expended in regards to the layout and decoration of this modest chamber. I'm a little surprised to find it only slightly larger than my own. Like mine, it's equipped with not a single window, being wholly interior. The impact of the place, on the other hand, could hardly be more different. The furnishings are not excessive, nor are they particularly opulent, yet still I find that they impart a sense of overwhelming exaltation. Every item, every surface, every convergence of light and shadow screams out 'Agata' in a tongue at once magnificent and vulgar.

The bed, to start with, is nothing to speak of, though the headboard is imposing and austere. It consists of a single plate of solid iron with circles of brass placed at regular intervals. It seems to radiate a continual barrage of arduous aetheric force. The space is thoroughly saturated with its exacting influence. It imbues the room with a discernible vibration very similar in quality to that of Agata's presence. Above the headboard hangs what is arguably the centerpiece of the entire house: a slightly convex oval mirror, just like mine, topped with a similarly sculpted eagle, yet the head, or heads as the case may be, have been broken off at the neck. Here, indeed, is my inverted crown, my headless sovereign, my acephalic imperial. I can't help but wonder if there's a companion piece in Vital's room as well.

That the piece is broken, rather than headless in design, is beyond question—the break is jagged and uneven and looks blatantly conspicuous. It looks as if it's been wrenched off its body by an especially strong pair of hands. I can only imagine it was Agata who did this. The lamps to either side of the glass emit a reserved and furtive light as if sworn to secrecy regarding the details of the crime. I hadn't thought of it before, but the shallow curvature of the two mirrors, hers and mine, seems specifically designed to capture every inch of their containing rooms.

Two narrow desks of stained mahogany run parallel to the bed on either side. The one to the right, if one is facing the mirror, supports a cluster of photographs set up in small, silver frames. Their subjects, most of whom are carefully posed, bear a notable resemblance to Vital (more so than his sister). This is true at least in spirit, if not so much in their physical features. There are particular qualities, on the other hand, that run through them like a theme: a subtle appearance of criminality, a tendency to spite the camera, an elusiveness of character that suggests the regular assumption of multiple conflicting roles. Some are clearly of the upper classes while others appear far more rough. The variety found among them is remarkable.

The photographs themselves appear to be of considerable age. Five slender candles, burned to various lengths, have been carefully arranged among them. Though it holds to no discernible pattern, the elegance of the display speaks to a hidden symmetry. I've swapped two of the pictures with one another. I simply couldn't resist. Isabel and I have already begun to do the same with some of the more insipid paintings on the walls around the house. We've agreed to continue to do this as the whim inspires us.

The other desk is far less cluttered. A fairly modern radio sits on one corner against the wall. It's not a particularly elegant model—a copper mesh screen and white-painted frame, a dial for tuning and a dial for volume, major stations printed right on the glass below the corresponding frequencies: *Luxembourg, Lyons, Midland, Brussels*. On the other end lie two hardbound books stacked one atop the other. The first appears to be a study of ballistics among a wide range of heavy artillery. The second, so old that it's falling apart, comprises the memoirs of a Countess Potocka of Poland. My interest is more than a little piqued by the latter, yet I'm afraid to lay a finger on it. Putting it back exactly as it is would be no easy task.

More curious still is the stack of white paper on the center of the desk. There are eleven sheets in total, each of them covered with endless marks drawn in bright red ink—a sort of swooping reverse 'S' with flourishes on either end. These are traced with the elegance of a well-practiced hand and arranged in neatly-spaced rows. In several instances, the characters are continuous, consisting of a single line from one to the next. Where this is the case, they progressively diminish in size, eventually trailing off before a new series begins. Some are crossed with a central stroke, though the majority are left unmarked. I can only imagine the mistress of the house sitting in her bedroom for hours on end, listening to the radio and consulting her book on ballistics as she perfects her technique of tracing meaningless red curves.

Despite the abundance of evidence, I think it highly unlikely that Agata is insane. I suppose it's possible that these things were set out and arranged specifically to baffle me. While this would fit quite well with Isabel's assessment, it would leave any number of things unexplained. My intuition simply won't allow me to believe it. If nothing else, I can hardly imagine Agata playing along with Vital's whims, if indeed they amount to nothing more than that.

I remain convinced that there's far more going on here than any single theory can encompass. The strangeness of my situation is so succinct that I can taste it. It saturates my senses and exhausts my curiosity. I don't suppose that I'll ever be given a reasonable explanation. Upon reflection, this might be for the best. There's a particular power awarded to those that can abide in total darkness. To partake of a mystery that one can't possibly hope to understand is an attainment in itself.

A few additional items remain as yet unnoted: a marble bust of a dire-looking man with his head wrapped up in an elaborate turban; a sumptuous nightstand draped in fine, silver lace; a large, framed painting of a ruined fortress along with several smaller works of art; an empire-style armchair on which I recline as I write this entry. The space is equipped with an actual closet, which eliminates the need for an armoire. Further, in addition to the mounted lamps that flank the mirror, a monstrosity of frosted glass hangs from the center of the ceiling. The light that pours from its ample bowl is so soft that it does little more than accentuate the shadows. The thing reminds me, more than anything, of Agata herself: dimly radiant, of considerable girth, and completely overbearing.

I purposely brought nothing with me to amuse myself aside from the single notebook page. While the prospect of remaining awake for a night in an unfamiliar room sounds like the very soul of tedium, I've become so enamored with this house and its mysteries that I can hardly imagine a more enthralling way to spend my time. I have reason to believe that my courtship with the house is still in its early stages. There are subtle rhythms I have yet to internalize, unobserved routines I have yet to uncover. I may never come to know precisely what it is that's going on here, yet the furnishings themselves pass on subtle enigmas that are worthy of diligent study. What better place to absorb these ciphers than the sleeping chamber of the house's mistress?

3:21 a.m., by the clock upon the nightstand

I've switched on the radio in order to introduce some variation to the presiding monotony. While changing the station seems ill-advised, I've turned the volume down nearly as low as it will go. The needle is set just to the left of *Sterope* (a third of the way between *Scottish* and *North*). The periodic swelling of a barely-discernible orchestra pervades the overwhelming silence of the house at night. I hadn't expected to hear anything but static at so late an hour.

Thus far, I've limited my exploration of the bedroom to the contents of a single drawer. The urge to pry further burns within me like a raging pyre, yet I feel it's important to temper my imprudence. Curiosity is a potent force when it's held a little bit in check. In any case, it seems best to proceed with the utmost caution. I have every intention of following Vital's instructions in spirit if not to the letter.

The thought brings to mind a particular question that's been rattling around inside of my head—just how far over my boundaries am I expected to proceed? Vital has increasingly come to place his trust in me, yet I have every reason to assume that I'm expected to abuse it. I've been encouraged from the start, if only indirectly, to break implicit rules. It feels as if we're engaged with one another in a complex game of strategy, complete with sacrifices, bluffs, negotiations, and false leads, all of which unfolds upon a playing field that remains at least half-submerged in darkness. That his intentions still elude me is mitigated by the fact that I'm developing intentions of my own.

The drawer I chose resides in one of the desks directly below the radio. I was disappointed to find it very nearly empty, housing only a small collection of coins and a letter in an unknown tongue. The latter item, comprised of but a single page, is addressed directly to Agata. It's signed in a hand so painfully stylized as to be illegible. The coins were found concealed inside the letter, which was folded up in thirds. There are twelve of them, each completely different from the others in both style and size. Most of these are unrecognizable to me, though I think I can identify the Austrian *krone*. Every one of them, without exception, features a bicephalic bird in relief upon one side.

It's worth noting that the letter is stamped with one too, near the top. This particular version looks especially familiar. I think it comprises the coat of arms of some country or another—Russia? Albania? Montenegro? I don't know. The ink is impressed in vivid scarlet. Its wings and tail are lined with stylized feathers depicted in glorious, swooping curves. The two heads appear especially vicious, their beaks wide open and their tongues upraised as if to spite the sky. Above them hovers a blazing star with seven equidistant points. It's all very regal.

The drawer being duly explored, I've returned to my station in the armchair. Self-imposed restraint gives rise to the most scandalous temptations. I can think of one hundred petite transgressions and another twenty vile ones after that. The cadence of the music that proceeds from the radio, though it can only just be heard, exerts a vaguely hypnotic effect upon my impressionable mind. When combined with the monotony of my late-night vigil, this tends to make me prone to flights of fancy. I could swear, for instance, that the electric hum of the radio is particularly drawn to the iron headboard on the bed. From there it surges directly downward as if attracted by a presence in the bowels of the house. My attention is seduced by fantastical visions of color-coded, subterranean chambers, each of which is subtly imbued with an emanation from the crown. In my current state of mind, even the chair on which I sit appears to be implicated in the endless machinations of this place.

I straddle the line between a desire to distract myself and an even greater desire to let the night have its way with me. I've read through the contents of my latest stolen page six or seven times at least. As with the others, it seems to comprise little more than an outline of what is presumably a larger work, a gargantuan masterpiece so tenuous and catastrophic that it could never be committed to paper. My thoughts flit like a restless sparrow from one thing to another. Given what I know about the layout of the house, I try to imagine where Agata might be hiding herself. So far as I'm aware, there are two types of vigil, both of which involve remaining awake throughout the night. In the first, one maintains a close watch over something that presumably needs to be guarded, while in the other one devotes oneself to a continuous stream of unceasing prayer. I somehow imagine that Agata's managed to combine the two.

As the night wears on, the radio periodically drifts from one station to another and back again. Fragments of speech occasionally break through the rolling strings and woodwinds. The narcotic delirium that interpenetrates the house, especially in the later hours, seems to rise to a momentous peak within the confines of this little room. I'm vaguely aware of a persistent urge to give in to something that feels distressingly near—a lucid sleep of unchanging vigilance that awaits in the shadow of every passing second. Despite this sensation, or perhaps because of it, I'm given to an irritating restlessness. I really don't know what to do with myself.

Oh hell, I may as well investigate another desk drawer.

Moments later

Disappointment. Not a single thing inside.

4:57 a.m.

I've managed to commit the unpardonable sin of falling asleep at my post. Lulled into a gentle torpor by the mesmerizing rhythms of the music, I let my eyes droop closed for but an instant. Immediately as I did so, a pallid glow in the back of my mind rolled forth and pulled me under. I must have been out for a little more than twenty minutes. If not for the occurrence of a minor catastrophe, I might have slept through the remainder of the night.

Upon reflection, sleep may not be quite the right word for the state that overtook me. What I can say for certain is that I lost track of my surroundings. I'd been aware, for several hours, of an imminent lucidity of greater depth than that of normal waking consciousness. It's this that crept up like a thief behind me and robbed me of my watchfulness, replacing it with a deeper awareness that shifted my vigil from one plane to the next. I remember every moment of my lapse of duty in meticulous detail. I'll record it here for fear of forgetting it otherwise.

The effect of my trance was instant and total—within a couple of seconds, I'd lost myself to a pure and translucent interior glow. This quickly consolidated into a vivid reverie in which I resided in two places at once. One part of me was with Agata somewhere in the house while another part resided in an opulent hotel. My companion in the latter place was none other than the very countess that appears in Vital's books. We'd concocted a plan, the countess and I, using stolen blueprints and a rusty set of drafting tools—an eagle was to be set loose within the corridors on one of the upper floors at a propitious moment. Our hope was to sabotage an anticipated rendezvous between two high-ranking officials. Something went wrong, cacophony ensued, a mirror was cracked in half. The resulting split in the reflecting surface gave rise to unexpected shifts in the layout of the building.

While all of this was going on, I was simultaneously engaged in a subdued conversation with Agata. She was expressing her displeasure that my maneuvers in the hotel were going so hopelessly awry. She seemed to narrate the action in the distant locale. The events unfolded precisely as she mentioned them, thus the two different timelines were kept in strict alignment.

As she was speaking, it occurred to me to try to work out where we were within the house. We were seated on the floor of an octagonal chamber, the walls of which were largely concealed behind rough silken curtains. The single exception was an archway behind Agata's back, beyond which could just be seen the beginning of a well-lit corridor. The space was entirely unfurnished. We faced one another. A small, handheld mirror lay face-up on the floor between us. In its reflection, I could clearly discern the unmistakable features of Agata's bedroom.

"If you're not going to listen," reprimanded my hostess, "there's hardly any reason for you to be here with me, is there?" While my mind was elsewhere, she'd been outlining a second plan to mitigate the damage brought about by the first, while at the same time I'd been growing progressively lost within the reconfigured hotel. Her hand shot down like a descending dove and picked up the mirror by its handle. With two nimble fingers, she rotated it on its axis so that the reflecting surface was turned toward me. "The imperial has managed to find its way into the house," she said, as if it were a matter of little importance. "The stench of royalty will inevitably come to stain the furniture." With that, she firmly placed the mirror face-down upon the floorboards. Precisely as she did so, I was jarred out of my dream by a tumultuous burst in my immediate environment.

My first thought was that Agata had returned to catch me sleeping in her armchair. The noise was not unlike that of the slamming of a door. Bracing myself for a tense confrontation, I quickly confirmed that I was still alone within the room. I wondered if somebody had struck one of the walls from the other side, or if the sound had come from the slamming of a broom handle upon the ceiling of the room below. Only upon rising did I discover the culprit. The radio had died—the lights on the display were out and the speaker had gone silent. A moment's examination revealed the plug lying on the floor just beneath the blackened socket. Something must have gone wrong with the electrical current and blown it clean out of the wall.

I was hesitant to replace the plug lest I cause another explosion. I took a chance and pushed it back in place without incident, yet the radio remains inoperative. The scorch marks on the outlet can clearly be seen. I'm afraid the effects of my meddling hand will be all too visible when Agata returns. I'm not particularly bothered at having left evidence of my presence in the room. After all, I've been assured that I'm beyond accountability. Still, I feel that I've inadvertently betrayed my orders. I've failed to maintain my hold upon the space I was expected to keep watch over.

Agata's statement regarding the imperial still echoes through my thoughts. It's clear that she was referring to the bird that I'd conspired to let loose inside the hotel. Even with the radio off, I find myself inclined to fanciful ideas. I can't help but mark a difference in the atmosphere of the bedroom. The stench of royalty, as Agata termed it, seems to saturate the bedspread, the silver lace upon the nightstand, and the convex bowl of the overhead lamp. It rises from the headboard at the end of the bed like a churning cloud of vapor. This seems far more conspicuous than the blackened plug on the wall. What's more, I'm given to the inescapable notion that it's slowly spreading to every region of the house.

With that, I think I'd better bring this little night watch to a close. Quite enough damage has been done for one night. Dawn is still more than an hour away, yet I don't feel inclined to spend another minute in this place.

The stakes have been raised just a little bit higher. Vital has tasked me with an act of petty destruction that can't fail to have repercussions. There's a room in the basement, beyond the laundry station, that remains firmly secured when not in use. Of course, I'd come across it during my first week here and had written it off as inaccessible. I've been instructed to find a way inside, either by picking the lock or simply breaking down the door. Vital assured me that the latter is hollow and should give way quite easily beneath sufficient force.

I haven't the slightest clue how to pick a lock and have never attempted to break one. There's hope, I'm told, that I might locate the key, but even Vital doesn't know where it's kept. Though her name was never mentioned, it's overwhelmingly clear that the room belongs to Agata. I only hope to God I don't encounter her inside.

"Your presence in the room is the sole thing of importance," Vital assured me. "Once inside, you can do anything that comes to mind. Consider it a violation, an official act of trespass. There is a splendor to ignominy that few allow themselves to know."

I was given no precautions, nor a word of advice on my technique. I could easily dislocate a shoulder in a misguided attempt to force my way in. This is the least of Vital's concerns. He is anything but practical. He dispenses his instructions like a high-ranking official, never bothering himself with the details of their execution.

This notwithstanding, I find myself flattered by the weight with which he endows these directives. There's a feeling of being invested with a responsibility that lies beyond my station. None of this is diminished by the often petty nature of his requests. One wants so badly to trust him, to surpass his expectations, to conspire with him in his incomprehensible games no matter how absurd they might appear.

I can't help but suspect that the place I'm to trespass is none other than the "lower observatory". The thought of officially betraying Agata a second time leaves me surprisingly untroubled. She must know by now that I've set foot inside her bedroom. I've encountered her in passing on several occasions over the course of the last two days, yet she regards me no differently than before—without a trace of affection, like a mistress to her faceless servant. It seems I'm hardly even worthy of eliciting disdain. Perhaps she sees me as nothing more than a plaything for her brother. We'll see if she continues to tolerate his eccentricities after I destroy the lock on her door.

Rather than grill me for details regarding my previous directive, Vital proceeded to use the remainder of our session to reminisce about his childhood. "My father was in no way a religious man," he declared. "If there was a single thing he venerated, it was the exactitude of nature. The world, he maintained, while hardly fair, is unfailingly precise. He chose to emulate this quality with all the fervor of a cardinal. It was made known within this house that punishment would follow disobedience with a consistency that bordered on the mathematical."

A moment of silence passed between us. I hadn't the slightest idea what he was trying to tell me. The prospect of hearing him speak about his father was more than a little enticing. Vital rarely reveals anything of substance about his past.

"He used occasionally to offer me a sort of challenge," he continued. "If a particular misdeed is worth the consequences it incurs, so he argued, why not indulge it to the full? He all but dared me to openly defy him, knowing full well what would come of it. Of course, I could never bring myself to do it. I disobeyed him only when I knew I couldn't possibly be caught."

I'd been gazing at my coffee cup as he recited his little parable, tracing the play of the lights along the inside of the rim. Casting my eyes up to his own, I told him that I didn't believe a word of it. This clearly caused him some amusement. Little else was said between us for the remainder of the session.

What else might I relate here? My lapse of watchfulness in Agata's room seems to have done something to my perception. The flame that persists in the back of my mind has grown significantly stronger. In the quieter hours of the night it flares and hisses like a jet of gaslight, shedding its glow on a place inside of me that extends beyond the confines of my body. What I'd before perceived to be fleeting patterns, as of scattered fragments of wallpaper or upholstery, have since given way to the most tantalizing hints of doorways, corridors, stairways, and lamps. My perception of these things is more consistent than before, yet still I can never quite manage to fix my gaze upon them. They slip away before my scrutiny like oil over water.

These elusive visions seem to continue directly from my dreams, which, as of late, have largely taken place inside the grand hotel from Vital's magnum opus. A part of me seems to remain there upon waking, to wander without aim along its richly-decorated passages. This place, if it can be called as much, seems not so different from the house in which I live and work. While the latter lies outside of me, the former reaches inward. Thus do I stand like a pane of glass between two completely different worlds. As I pass from the parlor to the sitting room, I can't help but feel as if my movement through one of them somehow mirrors that of the other.

My one reprieve from all of this nonsense is Isabel's regular company. She keeps me relatively grounded with her superficial outlook and her perverse sense of humor. The woman will stop at nothing to amuse herself. This one redeeming quality comprises roughly eighty percent of her personality. I sometimes wonder whether she's more fit for my job than I am. At the very least, she could perform my duties with flawless impartiality.

She brought me my breakfast yesterday morning—cold cuts on rye over coffee. Her visit woke me at the ungodly hour of 3:30 in the afternoon. After we ate, we shared a cigarette and I told her about my vigil, omitting any mention of having fallen asleep on the job. She appeared absolutely mesmerized by my account of what I'd found in the bedroom. I was even able to detect a streak of jealousy.

"Agata's meaningless scribblings sound like a type of graphomania," she said as the cigarette was held upraised between the fingers of one hand. "You know, for a long time I thought she was completely mute. I was shocked when I first saw her admonishing the cook over some trifle. The prospect of a vigil seems almost painfully suspect. She's been known to disappear for days on end without setting foot outside the house. I think she simply secludes herself when her own self-importance becomes too overbearing."

I offered no response to Isabel's assessment, nor did I tell her about the latest task I'd been assigned. I'm tempted to ask if she's proficient as a lockpick, but I feel it best to keep the matter to myself. Anyway, she can't fail to hear me from her room upstairs if I'm forced to break my way through the lower door. Come to think of it, the same is true of Agata. I suppose there still remains some chance that it may not come to that. I'll give myself a day or so to snoop around the house in an attempt to locate the key. Failing that, I'll do whatever needs to be done.

I've undertaken an examination of the parts of Vital's office that I've heretofore ignored. Something akin to superstition had prevented me from doing so sooner. I'd noticed before, over the course of our meetings, the variety of books that line his shelves, yet I'd rarely paid them any attention, being exclusively drawn to the unlabeled ones. His collection largely consists of volumes on European history, along with technical manuals, atlases, and military handbooks. Nearly an entire shelf is filled with cryptographical monographs, including a thick book on steganography by a German Benedictine abbot. So far as I can tell, there's not a literary work among the lot of them.

The items found on Vital's work desk are a disappointing bore: financial statements, itemized receipts, legal documents, and reports, among other things. A more thorough investigation would be needed to ascertain how he supports the household. I'm not inclined to make the effort nor do I particularly care. The map chest, on the other hand, has proven of definite interest. Roughly half of the drawers are filled with richly-colored city maps—Riga, Gdańsk, Königsberg, and others. Almost all of them are decades old, often with multiple versions showing different eras. These are interspersed with silken banners of scarlet, gold, and purple sewn with an entrancing variety of imperial arms. These latter items are so dazzling I felt compelled to take them into my hands.

The contents of the map chest, as with so many things throughout the house, are bound by a particular aesthetic. The residue of history is stained with dubious associations. Motifs appear only to vanish again, flitting from one place to another like a flock of restless birds. I'm increasingly convinced that a single phenomenon stands behind every variation of the imperial eagle. I can feel it in my marrow, yet it eludes my understanding. Vital had mentioned, during my interview, that his office contained items "of considerable worth". I don't know if he was specifically referring to these banners, though I hardly imagine he expected me to steal one.

Enticed by my findings, yet far from sated, I returned to the unlabeled books. As I cracked the cover of one of the later volumes, I was surprised to find a sparsity of actual text. Scattered headings and fragments appear amidst long spans of emptiness that dominate the page. The unfilled spaces look like lengthy bursts of static, vaguely suggestive of radio transmissions picked up by a barely operational receiver. The cryptic phrases dispersed among the silence are as portentous as ever, weaving a tessellated sequence of baffling permutations and narrative reversals. Vague references are made to a multiplicity of scattered incidents—an explosion on a balcony in an opera house, the assassination of a mirror image of the archduke of Milan, a letter poisoned with sap distilled from the center of the earth—every line of which is brimming with the usual intimations of royalty and treachery.

I couldn't help but steal a glance through the books that follow in the series. They grow progressively destitute, the later sections containing only the occasional cluster of text. The same is true of the majority of the initial volume. It's as if the text emerged, little by little, from an oblivion of unconsciousness, only to retreat back into its source as the narrative exhausted itself. More often than not, the words in the more sporadic sections run together into long and unintelligible compounds. I'm reminded of the barbarous names found in the incantations of the ancient Greeks. The empty spaces in-between emit a tangible essence from the surface of the page, an unseen radiation that seems to seep into the atmosphere and contaminate the shadows.

Before leaving the office, I thumbed through the final book. Scarcely a word can be found between its covers. I'm inclined to believe that this one comprises the crown jewel of the entire series. The resonance with which the pages are suffused seems indifferent to what's written on them. It's as if the compiling of the text were a sacramental act to which the content is only secondary. It seemed especially sinful to deface this one, yet I felt it a dire necessity. Putting prudence to one side, I tore a single page out from its bindings. I took it with me into the closet for the duration of my shift. I clutched it like a fetish as I peered through the glass, two fingers gently stroking its surface as it lay pressed against my breast.

27 January

The deed has been accomplished. The door has been breached. The room that lies beyond has been exposed before my eyes. My efforts to locate the key having failed, I was forced to proceed like a savage. I made use of the urn that sits on the mantelpiece as a makeshift ram, repeatedly slamming its base against the wood both above and below the lock. Before doing so, I took the liberty of emptying its contents. What better place to do this than in the hall before the door? So far as I know, the disordered pile remains exactly where I left it: playing cards, cigarettes, flowers, fireplace ash, silverware, ground pepper, and other detritus. My iron bludgeon was heavy enough to cause substantial damage to its target, though it nearly ripped my arms out in the process. Its handles were so damned abrasive that they made my fingers bleed.

After a quarter of an hour, the door began to give way. A light shone through from the other side as the wood began to crack. I relentlessly attacked the weakest points in the hope that it would break around the deadbolt. Once it had sustained sufficient damage, it was easy to force inward with a firm kick of the heel. Having let the urn drop with a resounding clang, I paused for a moment to catch my breath. Already, the ambient spirit of the house had begun to surge through my body in pulsating waves. Through the half-open door, I could just make out the folds of a heavy, silken curtain, its surface adorned with sinuous blossoms of pale gold on olive.

Attracted by the colors, I stepped inside to find a chamber that was roughly the size of Agata's bedroom. Precisely in the center stood a slender table with curved wooden legs and a white marble top. From the handle of a drawer beneath its surface hung a long, crimson tassel. Thick, white candles on wrought iron stands were found to either side, their bases largely drowned beneath cascading pools of wax.

A section of the far wall was concealed by the silken curtain. In the ample space between this and the table was found the centerpiece of the entire room—a throne-like chair fashioned from rough-grained wood and painted a uniform slate-gray. White leather cuffs had been affixed to the arms and the two front legs, each equipped with a copper buckle and a strap lined with tiny holes. The piece betrayed a primitive aesthetic that was conspicuously out of line with the rest of the décor. It was clear that it had been assembled by an unskilled hand. At a glance, I could discern that even the buckles were slightly crooked.

A length of smooth, white fabric, folded back on itself, lay draped over the top. Upon closer examina-tion, this proved to be a sort of hood or mask. It was equipped with not a single aperture and was designed to fit over the entire head. What was presumably the front side was largely taken up by a detailed print of an eagle with two heads. This particular specimen, rendered in iridescent gold, was every bit as imposing as the others found throughout the house: down-turned wings with feathers like inverted blades, talons extending toward the base of the garment, beaks agape as if the bird were in the grip of a spasmodic fit of ecstasy. Between its dual crowns hovered a blazing red star positioned directly over the wearer's brow. A strap and buckle had been attached to the collar to ensure an especially cozy fit.

It occurred to me, as I admired the heavy wooden chair, that it couldn't possibly be used by just one person alone. There's no way, in other words, that Agata could strap herself to the device unaided. I found myself wondering precisely what type of salon she used to host back in her socialite days. Further, assuming that the thing was still in use, it followed that Vital must have something to do with it. The fact that he doesn't keep a key to the room only added to my perplexity.

Forcibly turning my attention from the throne, I proceeded to the curtain. I pulled it back to find yet another surprise awaiting me. Behind the heavy, flowing silk resided a panel of black iron that stretched from the ceiling to the floor. Such was its devastating impact that it nearly knocked me backward. A magnetic flux seemed to rush through my body, causing my heart to palpitate a little. Had the candles been aflame it might have damned well snuffed them out. If the headboard on Agata's bed is austere, this slab of naked metal was nearly unbearable. I immediately let the curtain fall back into place. The lush aesthetic of the latter seemed to counteract the overwhelming effect of the monstrosity that lay directly behind it.

Pressing ever onward in my exploration, hardly daunted by my findings thus far, I moved on to the table in the center of the room. The inside of the drawer revealed three thick stacks of paper along with a bottle of red ink and a metal-tipped pen. The latter was topped with a feather of deep burgundy attached with an ornate silver clasp. The pages were remarkably similar to the ones found on the desk in Agata's bedroom, but for the fact that their content was a little more elaborate. The looping reverse 'S'-like shapes that flowed across the paper tended more often than not to give way to discernable phrases. Where the words at first tended to run together, they quickly progressed into more reasonable sentences. I spread several of the sheets on the marble before me and examined them beneath the glow of the lamp, regretting the fact that I hadn't thought to bring my journal and a pen. I think I can reproduce some of the passages from memory. If I err in their reproduction, I can at least record the spirit of the text.

. . . *thecountessthecountessthecountessthecounting marks and double-crosses on a fraudulent receipt replete with flagrant violations in a desolate retreat*

. . . *summermoonlightqueendevouring scouring pieces of a puzzle never muddled with an eagle on a steeple in the middle of a neatly severed line*

. . . thesensethesensethesenseofanimpending feast be-
neath the banners of a blasted obsolete before the throne-
unending sleepsleepsleep upending in the deep

There were easily several hundred such phrases in a vaguely similar style, each beginning with a few rows of scribbling and abortively ending mid-sentence. These were interspersed by sections of variable length in which the stylish curves continued unbroken, either joined one to another or separate.

There I stood before the table, a handful of papers spread out before me in the gentle embrace of the ambient light. All the while, I was distinctly aware of another version of myself, an imaginary doppelgänger whose body overlapped with mine yet who resided in a remote locale unreachable from my own. The up-turned bowls of crystalline lamps, elaborately fashioned wall panels, and an exquisite carpet overwrought with arabesques appeared like faint reflections on a window at the back of my perception. As ephemeral as my double was, and as tenuous was her environment, their reality was as unquestionable as the marble surface beneath my palms. This other woman was at once myself and not myself. She was my sister in bicephalia, her heart inseparably joined to mine, her point of view comprising what amounted to a second head. It was not the first time that I'd noticed her, yet she seemed especially distinct in this place. Something about the content of Agata's papers seemed to render her more palpable than she is at other times.

73

These thoughts were distracted as I turned my gaze back to the gray-painted chair on the far side of the desk. I felt an irrational urge to recline upon its seat, to slip my arms and legs into the white leather cuffs, to fasten the straps as much as I was able to without the aid of another. The thought of the restraints tightly wrapped around my flesh exerted a fascination over me that I found nearly irresistible. To don the hood and tighten the collar while bound to the device seemed tantamount to nothing less than the exalted kiss of royalty. Before I could step out from behind the table, I was frozen in place by a familiar sensation. I thought at first that the curtain had fallen and the panel of lead exposed once more, only this time the rush of over-whelming severity passed through me from behind. I hardly needed to look over my shoulder, knowing exactly who I'd find there. I turned around to find Agata confronting me amidst the ruins of the door.

The taste of copper in my mouth rose to such an unpalatable degree that I'm afraid my face betrayed a less than dignified expression. Agata's body was fabu-lously draped in an elaborate dress replete with buttons down the front, the fabric adorned with a floral pattern in viridian and jade. Her eyes briefly turned downward to the still-intact deadbolt. "How very clever," she remarked, as if in observance of my penmanship or something equally puerile. She shifted her focus to the papers behind me. I realized that I'd been desperately trying to conceal them with my body, though my vain attempt to do so had been entirely unconscious. "I ap-pear to have interrupted a matter of importance," she remarked, her speech afflicted with a curious strain as if her tongue were half-asleep. I wished for nothing more than to disappear, to slip away into the habitation of my second self and to take refuge in its overwhelming opulence. However vehemently Vital might defend me, I was mortified that I'd been caught in the act of such a blatant indiscretion.

In the midst of my self-consciousness, I was put in mind of a curious thread that ran through nearly everything that I'd discovered in the house. Agata's nearly intolerable presence compelled me to confront her. "The unlabeled books in Vital's office," I began, having no idea how I might finish the sentence. This seemed to capture her interest. Her spacious brow grew furled. She regarded me as if amazed that I'd been so audacious as to speak before her. We stood and stared at one another for an unbearable span before she finally broke the silence. "What of them?" she returned. "I dictated most of their contents myself over the course of an excruciating fourteen days."

One thousand thoughts rushed through my mind, yet not a single one was conclusive. A feeling akin to jealousy flamed like a secret sin inside my heart. Something about what she'd said had struck me as inexplicably offensive. I simply couldn't bring myself to let it stand unchallenged. "But surely you were not the author," I asserted, feeling as if I were speaking on the behalf of the Imperial himself.

"The oracle passed through my mouth, if that's what's in question," she replied. "Its source is another matter entirely." From her tone, it sounded as if she were pointing out a grammatical error or a legal technicality in a document submitted to her. "Now, get out of my room before I throw you out," she added. "Vital's little games are all fine and good, but I can only be expected to put up with so much."

I could no more disobey the woman than I could walk through the walls. She granted me the courtesy of stepping aside so I could pass into the hallway unobstructed. I hastened through the ravaged doorway, leaving the pages haphazardly strewn across the table. My heart nearly convulsed as I passed beneath the unflinching gaze of the woman that was apparently my adversary. Having retained a fraction of my wits, I picked up the discarded urn and promptly returned it to its place upon the mantelpiece upstairs. It resides directly above me now, a little worse for the wear, but one hardly notices beneath the dim lights of the parlor.

Several hours have gone by since the events described above took place. The house has returned to the magnificent quietude that envelopes it throughout the smaller hours of the night. My nerves, as well, have settled down, though my confrontation with Agata still riles me. The presence of my interior twin has grown so thin as to be nearly invisible. The impressions that arise in my inner vision are anything but constant. They tend to fade in and out like images projected by a film strip before a faltering bulb. Throughout it all, the flame inside me persists with the steadfastness of a sentinel. It always illuminates something. I'm never left completely in the dark.

Lounging in the ground-floor parlor, from where I write this entry, I catch the occasional flash of brown and white across the surface of the mirror. A similar sight surprised me in one of the upstairs mirrors earlier this evening. The impression given is not that of a reflection, but rather something underneath the surface of the glass. My intuition tells me it's no less than the imperial—the eagle that escaped from the hotel during my dream in Agata's armchair. It can occasionally be seen flitting back and forth behind reflective surfaces, as if it's somehow become trapped in a phantasmal region that underlies the house.

I'm reasonably certain that the eagle's not supposed to be here. I fear that its presence beneath the glass is a result of my previous lapse of attention. My moment of negligence abides in my conscience like a black mark in a dossier. What's worse is the impression that I failed tonight's directive as well, that there was something that I might have done to prevent my being caught in the act. There are bound to be consequences, though I have no idea what their nature. It seems entirely possible that they'll unfold over the coming days without my even being aware of them.

It's late. Sunrise is swiftly approaching. I'm not quite moved to return to my bedroom. Perhaps I'll spend the remainder of the night in this nice wicker chair beneath the muted splendor of the lamps. After all, I can't think of a single reason not to sleep precisely where I please.

I managed to lose myself completely this evening as I gazed through the mirror into Vital's empty office. My nightly surveillance has increasingly grown to become an exercise in derangement. The red tint of the glass lends the likeness of a jeweled miniature to the space that lies less than an arms-length before me. The illusion distorts my perception of distance, causing the office to appear impossibly remote. My sense of embodiment diminishes to almost nothing as I contemplate the enigma. After little more than a quarter of an hour, I feel as tiny as a mustard seed.

This familiar sensation had just taken hold of me when I was startled by the unmistakable sound of a deadbolt sliding into place. My physical surroundings swiftly returned as if I'd been jarred out of a dream. Lifting my brow from the surface of the glass, I turned my attention to the door behind me. Its surface was awash in a feeble crimson glow that shone through the back of the mirror. I'd noticed early on that the closet door locks from the outside. What possible utility this might have is as perplexing as everything else about this place. I was hesitant to try the handle, having no desire to confront whoever awaited me in the corridor. The thought of spending the night confined inside my tiny cell seemed almost comforting in comparison. I was almost relieved when the door refused to open.

The certainty that it was Agata that resided in the hall was so succinct that I could feel it in my fingertips. I could hear the sound of her slightly labored breathing, though the real telling factor was her overwhelming presence. It filled the tiny closet like the intoxicating scent of an ancient, drunken beast. As if drawn to the unyielding defiance of her nature, I took a step toward the door and pressed myself against its surface, my palms placed flat against the painted wood while one temple rested beside them. Thus protected, I was able to indulge in an intimacy that I could never allow myself otherwise. Both of us partook of an unlikely communion though neither of us let our guard down. Something indefinable was passed between us, something vaguely untoward and disagreeable, a wordless acknowledgment tinged with a hint of confrontation, like a mutual exchange of veiled threats.

I scarcely dared to move a muscle for several exhilarating minutes. In time, feeling that I'd had enough of our encounter, I stepped away from the door and returned to the glass. Whether Agata would deign to set me free from my imprisonment was completely outside my control. This I accepted with a calm resignation, determined not to let the matter vex me overmuch. To so completely surrender my immediate fate was a luxury I'd rarely had the opportunity to taste. Set free from all considerations, I abandoned myself without reserve to the task that lay before me, feasting my gaze upon the features of the adjoining office with a lack of inhibition that bordered on the carnal.

The usual sensations stole over me like a swiftly spreading poison. My sense of self immediately vanished, my point of reference lost within the details of the office. The uncanny vacancy of the space on which I gazed took on all of the immensity of a force of nature. What had previously seemed almost painfully familiar appeared thoroughly inscrutable—an effect which I'd noticed several times before and which seems to come in alternating waves. My attention was absorbed by the pattern of the wallpaper to one side of the desk. For the first time, I realized that it was notably different from the styles displayed elsewhere in the house. The sinuous motifs, though entirely anomalous, were recognizable given a moment's reflection. The exact same pattern is found all throughout the hotel.

This, alas, was the last thought I remember before surrendering my self-awareness to my incorporeal twin. In the two days that had passed since I'd become aware of her in the lower room, I'd come increasingly to feel her continual presence. She resided like a sentry in the back of my mind. It was almost as if she'd been patiently waiting for the moment I relinquished control. I was more than happy to let her have her way with me. I trusted her as much as I trusted myself.

The precise sequence of the events that followed remains maddeningly indistinct. I seemed to have taken my place in the opulent hotel just as I had in my dream in Agata's bedroom, leaving my physical body behind me in the closet. I wandered through corridors made resplendent with gaslight, the effusions of the amber bulbs casting jeweled patterns on the carpets. I emerged at length onto an elaborate stairway that led down into a spacious lobby. It appeared that the hotel had been abandoned not long before I arrived there. Though they were largely in ruin, the furnishings were so opulent that I feared they might consume my senses.

Interior windows lined one wall above a row of white-paneled arches, the spaces behind them exquisitely lit and filled with scarlet banners and tyrannical busts. Several of the latter had toppled from their places, the fragmented ivory lying scattered on the tiles below. Long golden drapes had been torn down from their rods. Others were in tatters or were partially burned. The smell of smoke and burning fabric had been absorbed into the upholstery. Black ink and Beaujolais formed a haphazard mosaic across several of the walls. Furniture was overturned. The floor was awash with broken glass. Even the chandeliers betrayed the unmistakable mark of belligerent revolt. It looked as if the staff had conspired with the guests to unleash a minor tempest before moving on.

My sister-self knew exactly what had transpired throughout every region of the hotel. The memories washed over us like a fountain of excess: the extravagant parties, the secret meetings, the betrayal of official orders, the eruption of the crown into the fabric of the city and the convergence of disparate timelines. Precisely how we came to be involved in such an intricate fiasco was lost in a tangle of conspiracies and counterplots. Feeling as if I were late for an appointment elsewhere, I fled through the front doors into a desolate and timeless night.

Traitorous winds caressed my body as I made my way through long-familiar streets. The hub of the city shifted in accordance with an ever-changing regimen of scandals and insurgencies. I passed into a synagogue in which a dozen uniformed officials poured over out-of-date maps and ancient legal texts. A host of hanging bulbs shed their anemic light upon them as if to sanctify their efforts with the sweat of the Shekinah. I wound up making contact with an agent of the concierge amidst a group of aspiring poets. They lay asleep on their backs upon the marble tiles, their faces bathed in insupportable graces. I took care to step lightly as I approached my liaison. Fingertips touched fingertips. Passwords were exchanged. I delivered a message I'd received from the countess. The ex-hotel employee, so it transpired, having suffered uncountable deaths and resurrections, was holed up in a bathhouse in the administrative district at the other end of the city. He claimed to take his orders from the Imperial himself.

Having received a message in return, I emerged from the synagogue through finely-carved ivory doors. I crept through a city besieged by waters that rolled forth from a shore long lost to antiquity. The night-enwrapped façades had been ravaged not by moisture, but by the taint of regal influence. The populace had suffered uncountable shifts in the balance of power among emerging principalities. Alliances were confused; borders were uncertain; the prevailing zeitgeist had been thrown into disarray. The deluge exerted a devastating effect on the intrigues perpetuated by the city's intelligentsia. As I passed from one place to another, I caught occasional glimpses of the tangled threads at play. The pattern they wove revealed a perfect likeness of the two-headed eagle in its most treacherous aspect.

Several additional meetings followed before my sister in spirit at last relinquished her hold on me. Such was their complexity that the memories run together in a blur. I don't know how long I continued to keep my gaze trained through the mirror after returning to the tiny closet. Eventually, my body regained its sensation; the air I breathed was once again my own. When at last I stepped away from the glass, I was surprised to find the closet door wide open. I found this more startling than anything I experienced while I'd inhabited the body of my twin. I can't help but think of Agata standing behind me, her shadow falling over my incapacitated body. There is definitely an enmity between us now. That is no longer in question.

When I returned to my room, the clock on the nightstand confirmed that I'd been out for several hours. The sun is coming up as I write this. I'm not entirely inclined to sleep. I'm a little afraid that when I wake again the entire episode will appear as insubstantial as a dream. For now, the experience illuminates my memory with the immediacy of a flame. I feel a closeness with my second self which seems more essential than anything I've ever felt before. I don't want to lose this.

A little distance, on the other hand, has brought some clarity to the link between us. In hindsight, the dynamic seems perfectly obvious—if I cease to exist on one side of the veil, I cross over to the other. Under certain circumstances, I seem able to reside in both worlds at once. I'm only dimly aware of the criteria needed in order for this to happen. I feel naggingly certain that the answer to this problem lies in a single, mathematical key: the sum of all the ratios between obedience and disobedience, explicit and implicit rules, the bicephalic and the acaphalic, the house and the hotel.

Aside from this, few conclusions of substance can be drawn from my excursion. The rich perfume of treachery still enwraps my inner senses. I feel certain that my twin is protected in her travels by the mandates of the Headless One, a sovereign power that would seem to persist throughout all eras of history. Its reign is never-ending, its dominion unbroken, its influence made known in the official insignia of every nation in the world. Its jurisdiction knows no sides and suffers no allegiance. I can only speculate as to the role of this monarch in the war that Vital took part in. That its imprint was made known both in the trenches and the palaces seems overwhelmingly clear. Its authority is verified by the sheets of paper that lay concealed in my armoire, by the official emblems of empire and dominion, by the ritual corpus of the ancient Greeks, by the manifestos of Battaile, and undoubtedly by a host of other things that I have yet to become aware of.

2 February

Agata, at least for the time being, has been put into her rightful place. I found it necessary to repay her for the favor of locking me in the closet. I drafted Isabel as my accomplice. My armoire has been sacrificed. My uniforms are now laid out directly on the floor. As for Vital's pages, I have them safely concealed between my mattress and the bed frame.

We carried out our operation in the heart of the night while the household was still sleeping. Great care was taken to maintain relative quiet as we transported the armoire down the stairway. We maneuvered it, with both doors open, directly before the entrance to Agata's bedroom. A ridiculous display had been set up inside, at once an open provocation and an affront to common sense. It took several attempts to get the armoire into place without upsetting the precarious arrangement. At one point it very nearly toppled over on its back.

No sooner would Agata attempt to step out of her room than would she find herself confronted with the fruit of our labor. I'd retrieved one of the banners from Vital's map chest and hung it at the back of the interior, a dizzying arrangement of flaming white candles set up below its dangling golden tassels. In their midst stood a statue of a soldier on horseback, the plume of his helmet rising roughly to chest-height. The shimmering flames traced cryptic directives along the belly of the beast from below. Thick folds of drapery, borrowed from the upstairs dining room, had been affixed to either side, the ornate print of gold on deep crimson lending a hint of extravagance to our otherwise uncluttered display. Above and between the twin heads of the eagle that spread its wings across the banner hung a modest, gilt-framed mirror suspended from a slender twist of wire. A message—*THE CLEVER MAY SEVER THE ROOT OF ALL ENDEAVOR*—had been painted onto its surface, the letters reversed from right to left and painstakingly executed with a brush and black ink.

Agata's bedroom door opens inward. Despite her bulk, it's clear that she suffers from frailties of the body. There's no way she could move the thing without someone else's help—at least not without courting disaster. Our efforts were rewarded shortly before sunrise as we amused ourselves over cards and champagne. The corridors shuddered with a piercing exclamation that inspired us to raise our glasses. Not a word passed between us as we acknowledged the sweetness of our minor victory. Our success continued to grow all the more delectable as the initial shout was followed by several furious calls for Vital.

The day before, I'd taken the liberty of disabling the lock on the closet door. A quantity of melted wax in the deadbolt shaft should be sufficient to prevent it from sliding shut. Despite this precaution, I've no doubt that Agata will exact her revenge somehow. Her type never fails to reassert dominance after even the most minor indignity. It's possible that our mutual aggression will blossom into tacit war. I'm prepared to defend myself in whatever way proves necessary if it comes to that.

My nights continue to unravel like a roll of celluloid soaked in laudanum. Were it not for the clarity provided by Isabel's companionship, I fear I might slip into the perilous abyss between conjecture and hallucination. Waking and dreaming have become hopelessly entangled. My memories are prone to gaps that cannot be accounted for. I distinctly recall fleeing in the middle of the night with a bundle of pages from Vital's books. I can still smell the coffee in the late-night café I eventually took refuge in. Plans to use my stolen papers for unintelligible ends vied with an irrational fear of pursuit. I don't remember the details of my eventual return, yet here I am again. I don't know when exactly this could have happened. Perhaps I merely imagined it. Were it not for the calendar in Vital's office, I'd have long since lost track of the date.

Meanwhile, the mirrors continue to vex me in new and interesting ways. The imperial, so it transpires, is a master of evasion. I'll frequently catch sight of him in the glare on a reflective surface, always in my peripheral vision, usually perched on some item of furniture visible only through a doorway or around a corner. By the time I turn to the reflected image, he's disappeared again. I rarely catch more than a flurry of motion as he flees to some other locale. Further, he's taken to tapping with his beak upon the reverse side of the glass. He does this only when my back is turned. I suspect it amuses him to try my patience in this way. Given his size and obvious strength, it's only a matter of time before he breaks through into the house.

Since the time I wrote my previous entry, I've twice crossed over into the world of the hotel. This has only ever taken place as I've gazed through the mirror into Vital's empty office. I'm confident that I can make this transition whenever I desire to. I've managed to pinpoint a specific technique. Already, it's begun to feel perfectly natural.

The trick, it seems, is to identify completely with two opposing qualities at once, both of which are taken on by the office after a sufficient period of observation. On the one hand there's an unbearable sense of familiarity, and on the other an overwhelming feeling of estrangement. If I can manage to reside in the space in which these two things overlap, I find myself reduced to little more than an abstraction. It's as if every aspect of my nature is based upon a single, general principle, a basic formula so lightweight that it can slip free from its context. Making the transition from one world to another is a simple matter of reflection. My twin takes on the burden of my point of view like a second set of clothes.

Coming back to myself is another matter. Once I've vacated my body, my control has been surrendered. I merely have to trust that I'll be returned to my place in the closet at some point. My sister in spirit is possessed of abilities that I have yet to fully comprehend.

She's exceedingly clever, nearly impossible to read, and quite capable of adapting to continual upheaval. Thus far, I've been unable to discern her motivations. Her precise relation to the Imperial is impossible to gauge. I don't believe that she's bereft of ambition—for all I know she aims for nothing less than the crown. Like everybody in that world, she would seem to have an enduring place within the convoluted intrigues of the royal court.

With the onset of evening came my regular meeting with Vital. He didn't seem displeased in the least with the flagrant insult delivered to Agata this morning. If anything, I'm given the impression that our little prank amused him. Of course, he would never bring the matter up directly. It's far more in line with his general style to maintain a strict neutrality toward all extraneous affairs. He's incapable, on the other hand, of speaking without subtext. His most innocuous comments are like palimpsests. One could almost read them like a convoluted map.

"At every turning point in history lies an act of defiance," he noted at one point. He said this as if it were a casual observation, a matter at once trivial and apropos of my performance. "This is a matter of necessity, as inevitable as sunrise," he continued. "The machinery of destiny must occasionally be dismantled by the very operation of its parts."

I offered no response to his impenetrable statement. As usual, he hardly seemed concerned with my opinion. If anything, he appears primarily interested in the mere fact of my presence, as if there's something intrinsic to my basic existence that overrides whatever I might say or do.

Among the items that lay on the desk before him was an unmarked envelope of an inconspicuous size. He picked this up and held it between two fingers, its upper end casting an elongated shadow on the forms and receipts between us. "The crudity of your early directives might be viewed as akin to a sort of training," he said, his voice having taken on a more serious inflection. "You've proved adaptable enough. I'm more than pleased with your resourcefulness. I think it's time that we move on to matters of an altogether finer nature."

I kept my fingers neatly wrapped around my little teacup as Vital placed the envelope onto the desk before me. It was clear that I wasn't expected to unseal it in his presence.

"The instructions contained inside are mere suggestions," he assured me. "Feel free to elaborate upon any one of them as needed. There are subtleties to each of them that will reveal themselves as they're put into practice. Initiative will be required. Let your conscience be your guide. I trust you completely and feel assured that you'll arrive at the correct decisions."

The remainder of the meeting, as short as it was, was nearly impossible to bear. I was dying to know what diabolical schemes awaited me inside the envelope. Immediately as I returned to my room, I ripped it open along one edge. A single piece of paper contained a list of hand-written instructions, each one more perplexing and ambiguous than the last. *Light a fuse that burns more quickly on one side of the mirror than the other*, it began.

The items that follow read like aphorisms from a handbook of sabotage and insurgency. There are fourteen of them in all. I've read them over several times and still I fail to understand them. They're far too general to comprise directives in and of themselves. What might be derived from them is so vast in scope as to render them almost meaningless. *Let the enemy very nearly discern the pattern on the weave*, so I'm advised, *just before you set the carpet aflame beneath their feet.*

I won't transcribe the entire list within the pages of my journal—I feel that I must be cautious lest Agata break into my room and abscond with the book. The paper itself has been hidden in a place in which nobody is likely to find it. I'll include the final item just for the shameless pleasure of writing it down: *Unreflected light is invisible to the eye. Let this be your secret weapon.*

3 February

Something monumental happened during the hours after writing my last entry. As I reclined, half-dozing, against the foot of the main stairway beneath the apathetic splendor of the chandelier, I was given to a notion that seemed to demand an immediate response. I'd spent the majority of the evening immersed in contemplation of my new instructions. I'd hardly even bothered to keep track of the hour. "The stench of royalty," as Agata referred to it, had thoroughly interpenetrated every surface of the house. I rose from my place, having little reason to delay, and proceeded up the stairs to Vital's office. Availing myself of pen and paper, I began to compose a lengthy letter to the woman I've come to regard as my sister.

I wrote her concerning the state of affairs as they stand, at this moment, in the house. Further, I made mention of various details concerning the Treaty of Versaille, the October Revolution, and the opening events of the Spanish Civil War, all penned in a familiar and intimate hand as if I were writing of the details of my life to a loved one. I had just begun to describe the furnishings found in the chamber in the basement when the certainty again stole over me that I was being observed through the back of Vital's mirror. This time I could have no doubt as to the identity of my voyeur. The very woman to whom I was writing was watching me from somewhere in the distant hotel.

I rose from the chair and took myself before the mirror. *She* peered back at me from the image of my own reflection, her gaze as truculent as an infidel's. I couldn't bear to abide beneath her unwavering scrutiny for more than a few seconds' time. Just as I was about to retreat into the corridor, I recalled one of the directives found on Vital's list. While I'd best refrain from reproducing it here, I will mention only that it provided a key that I could never have found had I deliberately sought it out.

Within seconds, I was in the closet peering through the glass. I'd been far too lazy earlier in the evening to appear there for my nightly shift. It took no time at all for me to slip out of my body, the transition taking place almost entirely without effort. Reduced to no more than an infinitesimal point, I felt as cold and remote as an emaciated star. As it happened, my twin did not await me on the far side of the threshold. In the wake of her absence, I passed into an expanse of pure, unrelenting sovereignty.

The naked splendor of the imperial crown was almost too much to bear. Along with everything else, my very trepidation was swiftly drowned beneath its impossible glory. It swallowed my capacity for self-reflection, negating not only my history but all indignities to come.

Nothing could abide for so much as an instant in its timeless expression of inflexible authority. My hope had been to turn one mirror toward the other and observe their mutual reflection. Instead I came to assume the throne of a monarchy that knows no bounds.

My abduction continued for what seemed like an eternity. In a sense, I remain there even now. It's as if some part of me, having undergone the coronation, must ever continue to uphold the scepter lest the reign of the monarch be broken. In any case, it was not I who wore the crown. I hold to no illusion of personal attainment. The true Imperial cannot be debased by something so vulgar as identity. The head that ceases to exist, being absolute and universal, belongs to everyone and nobody alike.

The events that followed my return to myself have been scoured from my memory. I must have staggered back to my bed at some point, too dazed by my experience to register the fact. I woke, as usual, with the setting of the sun, my midnight ascent still fresh in my mind. A string of additional memories would seem to have surfaced along with it—half-formed recollections that lie just on the edge of cognizance. These have the dubious substantiality of sequences from a dream, yet I can't quite bring myself to doubt them.

Among other things, I distinctly recall seeing the eagle in the house. It flew up the stairs into the second dining room, nearly colliding with the lamp that hangs above the table. The grandeur of its exalted office was carried in its bearing. Like the icon that prevailed on the banners of Byzantium, its appearance was an emblem of an authority that never rests.

Further, I feel fairly certain that I shared a meal in the downstairs dining hall with no less august a personage than the countess. The cook had conspired to prepare a minor feast for the two of us alone. I don't recall thinking it at all unusual that she would appear before me in the flesh. We spoke of secret cabals, murderous counterplots, and the infernal machinations of the concierge. There are other things that transpired as well: a peacock preening in the parlor; the porter banging furiously on the office door; a querulous assault with a flaming candelabra and the staining of a guillotine with wax. It's impossible for me to say whether these events truly took place. Though their timeline is a little hazy, they seem as real as anything else. Their ambiguity hardly sets them aside from my other experiences. Everything that goes on in this place feels as insubstantial as the wind.

My current theory is that these memories are not my own at all, but rather that they belong to my duplicitous twin. It seems reasonable to assume that she can take her place in my world just as I can cross the boundary into hers. When I step into her body, I'm no more than a passenger looking out through her eyes as she carries out her own agendas, while she, for her part, could well be capable of taking full possession of my senses. This would certainly explain my fragmented memories of what transpires while she's here. She's far more adroit than I could ever hope to be. I suspect that

I leave myself wide open for the taking when I make my transition through the back of the mirror.

The more I think about it, the more likely it seems that it was she that was behind my recent excursion from the house. Perhaps she intended to employ Vital's pages as passports through an unfamiliar world. I'm inclined to believe that this kind of thing will continue long after I've left this place behind me. The prospect doesn't cause me the slightest apprehension. It feels almost as if I'm fulfilling a familial bond. To allow my sister to pursue her objectives both in this world and her own is a distinction I would trade for nothing.

Speaking of leaving, I've come to the conclusion that my days in this house are numbered. I can scarcely imagine giving up my position, and haven't the slightest clue where I might go, yet I no longer think it appropriate to remain here on an indefinite basis. My communion with the Headless One has drastically changed my perspective. Where could I possibly go from such exalted heights? What more can I aspire to? It would be ill-advised for me to remain for too long where the apex of my work lies behind me. Yet another cycle must begin, something that follows on everything I've done here. The longer I stay, the more I'll risk succumbing to complacency. I have plenty of money, having been paid quite handsomely during each of my weekly meetings. It would be far better to leave than to degrade my position. It feels as if my tenancy has fully ripened and is just on the verge of falling from the tree.

Perhaps I'll abscond in the middle of the night without a word of explanation. What better way to conclude my time here than to mysteriously vanish? This would fall perfectly in line with the trajectory of everything I've carried out so far—one last act of irrational defiance, a final proof of the veracity of Vital's methods. Regrettably, there are several things that I'll never come to know. I could kill to find out the origin and context of Vital's unlabeled books, for instance, or the true intent and meaning of my employment in the house. On the other hand, my ignorance could well work in my favor. Not-knowing could be likened to the "unreflected light" referred to in my last directive. This is at once my secret weapon, my invisible ally, and my means of emancipation, its purity foretold by the empty pages toward the end of Vital's books.

Postscript

A sufficient period of time has passed since I penned my last entry. Much has happened in the meantime that has no place in this journal. For the sake of completeness, I'll pick up on the evening a few days after my encounter with the sovereign. Nothing of tremendous importance had transpired in the time between.

Some time after waking, upon stepping out to use the washroom, I was treated to the muffled echoes of a minor dispute. The voices emerged from Vital's office, which lay just around the corner at the head of the main stairs. Agata's was the most easily discernible of the two. It was clear that she was standing just beyond the closed door. It's exceedingly rare that she and her brother have reason to speak to one another at all. Filled with burning curiosity, I remained exactly where I stood and endeavored to take in every word.

Though their terse exchange was somewhat distorted, I was able to make out nearly everything they said. Agata was evidently displeased about something. Her tone was as stern and exacting as a whip. "The situation is not hard to understand," she insisted with a measure of contempt. "I've had enough of this indignity and I want that creature out of our house."

"There's nothing to get worked up over, Agata," returned my employer in a reasonable voice. "I have every intention of doing what needs to be done. The matter will be taken care of. I'll take things into hand. By tomorrow or the next day, you'll be free of the entire concern."

Their words coursed through me like the nectar of the gods. If I'd heard them as much as a few days before, I would have been perfectly mortified. I'd already made up my mind that it was time for me to go, yet I couldn't bear the thought of letting Vital down. His sister's sudden demand provided me with a perfect opportunity.

Fearing that Agata would soon step out into the hallway, I hastened back into my bedroom. I made a mental note to share a final drink with Isabel in celebration of my impending departure. Over the course of the next hour, I packed the single suitcase I'd brought with me when I moved in. Would I be afforded another shift in the closet? A further descent into the bowels of the war-torn city would form a reasonable pendant to my several weeks of blessed indolence. I expected that Vital would call a special meeting either later that evening or the next to inform me of my termination.

Still, the invisible flame within revealed enticing arabesques in the back of my mind. The lush euphoria that enwrapped my senses hadn't lessened in the slightest. Would it all come to an end when I stepped out of doors? The possibility seemed so remote that I didn't let it concern me. I imagined giving myself over to the wiles of my sister without condition or reserve, providing a permanent vehicle for her to occupy this world while I remained forever withdrawn in the imperial court. Such a luxury would so vastly surpass the pleasures of the house as to render them obsolete.

An hour went by, dinner was announced, I received no word from Vital. If indeed he planned to summon me to his office, he would probably wait until the following evening. Feeling emboldened by my impending release, I decided to do something I'd never dared to do before. I emerged from my bedroom, sauntered down the stairs, and proceeded directly to the dining hall. There, among the muted lamps, the candlesticks with gilt bronze flames, the woven screens, the statuettes, and the excesses of onyx, I sat myself at the dining room table directly across from Agata.

It would have been woefully ingenuine of her not to look up from her open book. I recognized the title by the condition of the covers—she was perusing the biography of the Countess Potocka of Poland. She regarded me with the supreme indifference of a sybil addressing her inquirer. Her vestments were deep blue this time, a rich and royal sapphire that lent an unexpected dignity to the lines that crossed her face. Her attention, as usual, was painful to endure. She exuded catastrophe like an opulent train wreck.

"All I ask," I said, nearly losing my nerve beneath the onerous weight of her gaze, "is that you answer for me a single question."

For a moment I was sure that she was simply going to stare at me, that she'd continue to maintain an uncomfortable silence until I got up and left her alone. I made up my mind to stand firm until the very end. I would refuse to leave the dining room until I received a proper response. "Go ahead and ask," she said at last with an air of casual indifference. "I'll tell you anything you'd like to know." Her fingertips remained impeccably poised upon the surface of the page.

After taking a moment to collect my thoughts, I did my best to express them as coherently as possible. "The events described in the pages you channeled," I began. "Can I assume these are an accurate reflection of Vital's experiences in the war?"

Genuine confusion crossed Agata's face. So far as I could tell, she was completely lost. "The war?" she asked as if perplexed by the term. "I don't know what you're talking about. Vital was never in any war. He was deemed unfit for military service."

I simply could not accept what she'd said with any degree of equanimity. My conception of Vital was inextricably linked to the narrative found in the pages I'd stolen. "I've seen an image of him in uniform," I pressed. "There's a photograph on the wall behind the door in his office."

"That's a photograph of our father," she returned. "*He* was a military man. Not Vital."

While I wanted to disbelieve her assertion, it didn't seem impossible. There was nothing in the photograph that suggested a particular time period. Could their father have provided the discarnate voice that had spoken through Agata's lips? Several things about the prospect didn't quite add up. The handful of pages that I'd taken from the books had clearly made reference to the First World War. Their father would have been far too old to be the narrator of that text.

Meanwhile, Agata had slowly come to understand what it was that I'd been asking. "You stupid girl," she said with unconcealed derision. "You really don't know a single thing. Have you read the books? *All* of them? Do you not understand their import?"

All I could do was stand my ground and maintain an icy silence. I felt as if my king had been put into check and there was little I could do about it.

"Are you aware of what lies behind Vital's endeavors?" she persisted. "You can't have failed to notice that the papers on his desk are several decades old."

I had, in fact, taken note of this, yet I scarcely grasped her point.

"I have no intention of interfering with my brother's measures," she said, her fingers pressing vigorously upon the surface of the page. "He has his methods and I have mine. We cannot possibly know what we unleash with our investigations. There are limits, on the other hand. We must hold ourselves accountable."

Her words sunk into the chambers of my heart like a stream of concentrated vitriol. Whatever theories I'd constructed regarding the books came crashing down like a house of cards. At the same time, though she regarded me with acrimony, I found myself luxuriating in her company. Something of the intimacy that I'd allowed myself to feel when she'd locked me in the closet had returned. In the midst of this sensation, I became aware of the unique opportunity that lay before me. Now that I had Agata's attention, I could ask her absolutely anything. However suspect her responses, they couldn't fail to shed light on the mysteries that vexed me. Just as I'd begun to formulate my words, my thoughts were interrupted by a tumultuous crash. The sound of shattering glass rushed through the air above the table like a train run off its rails.

The flow of conversation was irreparably severed. From the look on her face, I sensed that Agata knew exactly what had caused the disturbance. Whatever it was had enkindled her ire to an unacceptable degree. She rose from her seat and turned around, her physical bulk as oppressive as a citadel. "Oh, that impetuous bird!" she shouted with disgust before she stormed through one of the open archways. As if attracted by her magnetism, I got up from the table and followed in her wake.

I was greeted by the ruins of the central chandelier at the foot of the main stairway. A haphazard mosaic of glass and crystal had all but swallowed the pattern on the carpet. Perched atop the curves of brass that extended above the frosted lamp shades was the very eagle I'd set loose in the hotel. It was much larger in the flesh than I could possibly have expected. Its presence overflowed with an aristocratic grandeur that perfectly complemented the surrounding décor. I wanted at once to throw my arms around it and to fall down to my knees, but knew I must restrain myself. The magnificent bird appeared to gaze upon Agata with unconcealed spite.

"Vital!" screamed Agata. "Vital, get down here at once! I told you to get rid of this infernal creature!"

Such was the majesty of the imperial that I could scarcely take a breath. It turned its attention in my direction, its wings raising up as it shifted its footing. Its gaze passed through the veil of my flesh into the corridors of the hotel. I half-expected it to alight from its perch and fly right into me. Though I remained in its presence for no more than a few seconds, it was impossible to doubt what I was looking at—the herald of the headless god, the seal of the sovereign, the living icon of the greater Imperial that himself comprised the basis of the two-headed eagle in all of its manifestations.

Agata continued with her petulant tantrum until Vital was stirred from the comforts of his office. We passed by one another as he headed down the stairway. Neither he nor his sister seemed to notice my escape. I was determined to make use of the debacle as a cover. Here was my opportunity to slip out of the house. The time had come. I could feel it in my blood. The appearance of the eagle was both a confirmation and a warning.

A quick change of clothes behind the closed door of my bedroom was all that was needed to prepare for my departure. My suitcase awaited me by the bed, the pages stolen from Vital's books safely stashed inside. I swiftly crept down the narrow servant's stairway in the hope of leaving through the kitchen. From the sound of things, both Agata and Vital were still occupied with their minor fiasco. The cook had already left for the night and Isabel was nowhere to be found. There was not a single soul to witness my exit. If all went well, my disappearance wouldn't be detected until at least the following evening.

As I stepped out of the house into the embrace of the night, I immediately grew drunk upon the crisp evening breeze. The soft glow of starlight appeared so piteously gentle I could almost have broken down and cried. After spending several weeks indoors, the open sky was like a secret sin and I an adulteress of the highest order. I may have left the house on a previous excursion under the patronage of my sister, but to do so in full possession of myself was another thing entirely.

My passage was easy. I was carried by the wind. A brisk hours' walk took me back to the station on the outskirts of town. My fear of pursuit was as readily discarded as the clothing of a courtesan. After all, it was not as if I could be forced to return. My employment had always been a matter of choice. Would another woman take my place? Would the cycle begin all over again? Had anyone before me made it so far into the machinery of Vital's unfathomable process? Before another hour had passed, I was mobile again and these questions receded into the back of my mind.

As if in emulation of the imperial, I flew from the comforts of my nest to reside in a place entirely unknown to me. It felt as if I was turning my back upon my country of origin and abandoning the very place that had nurtured the person I'd become. This all took place a little over a month ago. The city I wound up in is not so far away. I speak the language, I have no need of a passport, yet I feel like an émigré in these unfamiliar streets. It's as if another war was waged during my season in Vital's employment and I've emerged from beneath his influence to find the world renewed by fire.

I've since taken a position as a daytime maid in the house of a family of little significance. I only work on a part-time basis, yet still I've found it trying to adjust to the rigors of real labor. In truth, my duties are fairly light. I learned from Isabel how to appear efficient with a minimum of effort. It's overwhelmingly clear that I'm an imposter in their world of respectability and decorum. I've become truly bicephalic, a mirror that reflects the light of two worlds at once, while yet another part of me remains ever uplifted in the ceaseless embrace of the Headless One. These very qualities have bestowed upon me a mastery of camouflage.

If there's anything I miss about the house, now that I've been away for some time, it's the easy conversations that I used to hold with Isabel. I suspect that I abandoned my station and duties at precisely the right time. I hadn't made mention of it in my journal, but I was beginning to feel a little bit restless. There's only so much snooping and lounging about that a person can reasonably stand. The place seems like a doll's house in the mirror of my memory—my nights a string of sapphire beads and my days stained with indolence. My hosts appear, in hindsight, more like principles than people. The entire affair has the ring of a game that I managed to win without lifting a finger.

There are several things I still don't know and am not inclined to pursue—what it was that Vital hoped to accomplish; the role of Agata in my approach to the throne; how, precisely, the countess and her retinue came to populate the pages of the unlabeled books. These things are little more than phantoms in the shadow of the crown. The latter abides in my reflection like an inversion of the mark of Cain. The distinction this bestows upon me is not devoid of purpose. The machinations at play in my sister's endeavors are all connected by a single thread. She collects the dictates of the sovereign and projects them back through an infinity of mirrors. Reflected also are the unspeakable keys to the rise and fall of empires. She has need of me. She employs me just like Vital did. There's an intimacy between us that allows for the consumption of an enviable sacrament. I, for my part, intend to provide her with everything she might require of this world.

A PARTIAL LIST OF SNUGGLY BOOKS